The Piano Lesson - Ashraf Ibrahim

Can life be disciplined between wrong and right, vice and virtue, black and white, like the keys of a piano? Or is there no escape from the devious and deceiving gray?

The

Piano Lesson

Ashraf Ibrahim

Author: Ibrahim, Ashraf.

Title: The Piano Lesson.

Publisher: Ashraf Ibrahim, 2021.

ISBN (paperback): 978-1-7775334-0-3

ashraf2183@yahoo.com

Front cover image © 2021 Freepik

First edition. 2021

Amazon Author Page: Ashraf Ibrahim

To my solitude, you are the source of my inspiration,
and you are the reason of my desolation.

Chapters

Ihab

"For me, the word 'hope' meant that you knew that there was something you would never have, but you insisted on holding on to it and hoping for it to happen, which was something that my mind, and the mind of any practical and balanced person, would reject."

The sound of my phone rose to the melodies of the wonderful piece of Liszt's music, 'La Campanella'. A magnificent yet extremely difficult piece of music whose beauty was complemented by the amazing and distinctive performance of the great pianist 'Lang Lang'. These charming melodies did not come from simplicity or ease, but rather are the result of musical notes that are very complex to read and extremely difficult to perform. They are the dream of every piano lover and the nightmare of every pianist.

La Campanella - Lang Lang - Franz Liszt

My love of 'La Campanella' together with my respect to the work of Liszt often stopped me from taking my incoming calls in order to continue enjoying that captivating music, which definitely deserved to be my ringtone. However, this time I decided to answer, it was Ihab; an old acquaintance from the days of my study in the conservatoire.

"Hamdi! How are you, my friend? I haven't heard your lovely voice in a long time."

"Ihab. How are you? I hope all is well with you."

"Listen. I didn't call you just to say hello. I'm having a big party at my house next Friday; a party that you must attend!"

"Ihab, you know me. I will promise that I will come and, in the end, I won't show up as usual."

"No, my friend! This party is different; this party is held for you! I've invited many music producers and artists, I even invited Hans Mulland."

The name took me by surprise. Hans Mulland was one of the best and most skilled pianists in the world, he was a great musician and a Grandmaster pianist in his days, and then he ran one of the biggest and most famous music schools for talented pianists from all over the world. His school ranked among the top music schools in the world, like the Juilliard School, the Berklee College of Music and the Yale School of Music. He helped talented pianists to complete their studies and refine their talents in his school, and then he introduced them to the world of classical music in the image that befits them as professional musicians.

I started looking at Ihab's invitation in a different way; one recommendation from Hans was enough to nominate me for top performances; this would put me in the ranks of international, well-known, pianists.

I answered Ihab in a low voice, "Hans Mulland! Do you think he'll come?"

Ihab broke into laughter, saying, "Now you give me all your attention! Oh, you mean! You declined my invitation, and I am your good friend, only to accept it when you know that Hans is coming. Yeah, he's definitely going to be there, he'll even listen to you play piano! I've arranged everything, you just need to come to the party and bring your magic fingers! Take care of their safety from now until Friday, or you'll have to play in front of Hans with your toes!"

Ihab continued to laugh, while I smiled shyly and said, "I will definitely come, and I'll bring my ten fingers with me. This is an opportunity of a lifetime. Thank you, Ihab."

The days passed slowly and laboriously. I was spending more than eighteen hours a day practicing and playing, and then spending the remaining few hours worrying and thinking. I gave my mind no time to rest and it didn't give me any time to sleep. What I said to Ihab was absolutely true; that was an opportunity of a lifetime; the opportunity that comes only once, and which may slip away from the unwary losers, leaving them in the muddy swamp of 'hope'. I've always seen hope to be the quagmire from which there was no way out or escape. For me, the word 'hope' meant that you knew that there was something you would never have, but you insisted on holding on to it and hoping for it to happen, which was something that my mind, and the mind of any practical and balanced person, would reject. Waiting for the results of any action was understandable, but to wait without work or effort, under the pretext of hope, was equal to stupidity. Hope was the muddy swamp of the disappointed, while work was the fruitful path of the diligent.

At eight in the evening of Friday, I was at the door of Ihab's house. I stood outside the garden gates for a while and took a look at the place, which was not a house in the conventional sense, but rather a big mansion with more than ten rooms that could accommodate a small legion with its horses. And the lush gardens that made it closer to an estate than to a house.

I saw Ihab in the garden, he hurried towards me with his big welcoming hug and wide warm smile as if he had not seen me in ages. Ihab was the living example of the 'good people'; handsome, polite, humble, and loving to his friends, especially the 'underprivileged' ones, like me. He began his training under the best piano instructors, who would come to his house as private tutors to teach him the piano, while I was training myself on a dilapidated piano in the school where my father used to work. When Ihab finished learning the basics of playing piano, his father rewarded him with a new 'Fazioli' to celebrate his 'achievement', while my mother sold the last piece of her jewelry to buy me an old piano with keys that had worn out and faded by the long use and the heavy hands of time. And while I joined the Conservatoire thanks to this old piano, Ihab joined the institute to study guitar! As he suddenly decided to learn guitar after he got bored of playing the piano, and to hell with the 'Fazioli'!

"Hey, my friend!"

The voice of Ihab in my ears and his hand patting my shoulder pulled me out of my memories. I smiled and opened my mouth to talk, but Ihab wasted no time; he grabbed me by the hand and rushed me into the house, telling me in a low voice, "Come on and meet Mr. Hans before he gets surrounded by the others."

I looked at Ihab and said, "Which others?!"

"Do you think you are the only one here who knows Hans and is looking forward to meeting him?! Come on, my friend."

We met Hans in the hall of the house, he was a smart-looking man of medium height, he had light hair, a trimmed beard, and a straight mustache. He looked more like a doctor and a scientist than the person of art. Ihab introduced us to each other in a few words. Hans greeted me with a wide smile, albeit with a piercing look from his blue eyes; a look I could not fault, I could see clearly that this was a man who should never be taken lightly. It was clear that Hans did not want to mix with any of the invitees, he was only coming to meet me based on Ihab's recommendation. That added to both my pride and anxiety. For Hans, I was the only guest, and the only one who would take the test.

Hans began to ask about music in our country in general, and about pianists in particular, then he asked me about my experience and ambitions, about my musical passions, and where I saw myself in the future. A few minutes later, Ihab shoved us into one of the rooms, it was clear that he had been instructed by Hans to keep the meeting short and not to let his time be wasted on frivolous and useless chatter. Indeed, the room we went to was the library, its walls were completely covered with books and volumes that reflected the wealth of its collector more than it indicated his culture.

In the middle of this room was the Fazioli! It looked like a piece of precious artifacts befitting the place, but for me it was the 'bench' of the exam, in front of which I would sit and answer, with my fingers, the questions and tests dictated to me by Mr. Hans.

Hans asked me to sit down, and I asked him in return, "Where do I begin?"

He smiled and said, "Play as you like."

I was so excited to play and so nervous to begin. I was not about to play and release tones and melodies out of the piano keys, I was actually about to knock on the gate to glory; the gate that stood between me and my seat among the great musicians in the world. Would that gate respond to my tunes and open wide? Or would it remain shut like the other doors I knocked and the other opportunities I missed in my life? I started with 'The Prelude' by Sergei Rachmaninoff, a difficult piece that requires tremendous skills and great sense of music. It is said that Rachmaninoff himself hated playing it! I put all my skills and senses into playing this piece and let my fingers tackle the piano keys with confidence and comfort. I wasn't afraid, I'm never afraid when it comes to playing piano, I just wanted to show him that I was a good pianist who deserved to join his school of gifted musicians.

I finished playing 'The Prelude' as perfectly as possible, looked at Hans, and saw on his face the expression of contentment and happiness, but I was surprised by his next request.

"Now play something from your country's heritage.

I love when talented musicians use their talent to promote their backgrounds and traditions."

It was a surprise to me, but I was ready. I began playing Omar Khairat's 'The Case of Amm Ahmed', one of the best Egyptian pieces written for the piano. It was composed by Omar Khairat, the Egyptian composer, pianist and conductor for a movie that carried the same name.

The meeting, or 'the test' as I saw it, lasted for more than an hour, and I was playing the whole time, so I did not notice the crowd that had started to leave the garden and come to the house, curious to know who was playing the piano, but Ihab stopped them from getting closer so as not to spoil the 'chemistry' that had begun to form between me and Hans during this hour.

Prelude in C Sharp Minor - Rachmaninoff

The Case of Amm Ahmed - Omar Khairat

After this hour of continuous playing, Hans moved towards me, put his hand on my shoulder, and clung to my hand with a smile while saying, "Goed, Goed." His praise was complemented by the reaction of Ihab's guests who applauded warmly and gathered anxiously around me, complimenting my performance and praising my work. However, I tried to get rid of them as quickly as possible so I could go back to talk to Hans, but I could not find him in the room, so I hurried to the garden looking for him, but still couldn't find him. Instead, I found Ihab standing with a group of his friends.

"Where's Hans?!" I nervously asked Ihab.

"He's gone," Ihab said, smiling indifferently, not knowing that by saying this he was throwing all my hopes and dreams into the bottomless pit of oblivion and despair.

I replied to Ihab desperately, "Did he leave just like that, without speaking to you or to me?"

Ihab replied with a calming smile, although it was not totally free of sarcasm, "Dear Hamdi, do you think he will take a contract out of his pocket and make you sign it? The man has listened to you play for an hour!

This is a sure sign that he likes you and likes your music. Calm down my friend, calm down. One of his associates will probably get in touch with you soon. Quit worrying and enjoy the party."

Having nothing else to say, I left Ihab and dragged my feet to one of the tables. I sat down feeling that the dream of being trained by Hans and joining his school was slipping from my hands and flying away, and that I was returning to the muddy swamp of 'hope', which erupted all the painful memories in my head.

The Family

"In Utopia, talent is man's way to glory, but in our world, it is man's way to madness."

My life has been a series of hopes and their disappointment, dreams and their brokenness, and wishes and their repression. This series was interrupted by moments of shock and tragedy that could break any man, especially those coming from families with more talent and fragility, and less resources and tenacity, like our family. My father was an art teacher, he missed the chance for private tutoring and the opportunity of finding a job abroad, so he settled in one of the narrow and dusty streets of the capital, struggling every month to survive on his meager salary. My mother on the other hand was a music teacher, she had great talent and greater beauty. But my father, the hard-headed and extremely jealous man from the south, wanted her for himself and only for himself, so he forbade her to work and kept her at home as a 'glorified' housewife, so she became a glorified and decent wife in a miserable and indigent house.

And in this indigent house, we were born. We were three siblings—me, my brother Hassan, and my sister Hanan. We were brought up on the richness of talent and the hardships of life, the blessing of the gift and the curse of poverty. Hassan inherited the talent of drawing and painting from my father, I inherited the love of music from my mother, and Hanan inherited my mother's beauty and charm.

Hassan was the middle child when it came to birth and number, and the first when it came to gift and temper. He was the most talented and the least patient among us. As if his blood was mixed with art and anger. He was in a state of constant and permanent revolt, a revolt against his teachers, a revolt against my father, and a revolt against even himself. He used to unleash this revolt together with his anger and frustrations not through his words or gestures, but in his drawings and art, all of which were extremely beautiful and absolutely crazy. His paintings were screaming with anger behind their calm colors, and threatening and intimidating behind their smooth lines. Hassan's professors took advantage of his madness to stop his progress and oppress his talent, so they gathered to downplay his work in favor of their cronies and their favored ones.

In the end, bias and nepotism triumphed over talent and genius, so Hassan's work was never given the chance it definitely deserved to see the light. He was not even appointed in the teaching staff at his own institute, and he did not have the opportunity to hold exhibitions, participate in well-reputed galleries or communicate with sponsors and supporters, so Hassan became one of the second-class painters who no one knows and no one cares about, despite the extraordinary talent of some of them.

Hassan remained stuck in the muddy swamp of hope, beating waves of disappointment and clinging to the glimmer of wishes, until that ugly day; the day when one of his professors who caused him not to be appointed as a professor in his institute came to our house, offering to take many of Hassan's drawings and works for a great amount of money. But, with one simple condition; the condition was that these works would no longer be my brother's property and would not be displayed in his name, but rather their lineage would pass to someone in the upper class. A man whose son decided one morning that he was a talented painter and that he must have his own gallery, which should show 'his own' work.

Hassan's delicate heart could not bear this deal or tolerate this offer. The man who once objected to his appointment to the institute of art under the pretext of his lack of talent came that day to buy his talent with a lot of money! He lacked talent as long as it was attributed to him, and he was all talented as long as it would be attributed to others.

Two days later, we woke up to my father's cry. Hassan was lying on the bathroom's floor, soaked in blood... Hassan committed suicide... He slit the arteries of his wrist, hoping that his talent that had always brought him misery would bleed out of his body with his blood, but that damned talent refused to leave his body before his soul, so the two went out together, leaving one dead body and one shattered family.

In Utopia, talent is man's way to glory, but in our world, it is man's way to madness.

For that family, it was all downhill from there. My brother could not bear the brunt of the injustice, so he chose to commit suicide. My father could not bear the brunt of my brother's suicide, so he passed away six months later, and my mother could not bear the demise of the two, so she passed away a year later.

The family was scattered between the lost paves and the darkness of the graves, leaving only Hanan and myself.

As for Hanan, she was the least talented and most intelligent among us, she killed any call within her to practice any kind of art or even learn it, and she relied on the weapon that never failed—her beauty. She 'targeted' one of her classmates and had him fall in love with her. She did not choose him because she loved him or even because she liked him, she chose him when she learned about his family's great wealth and the fact that they all lived abroad. The young man came here to get his Master's degree and then return back to take over his father's work abroad, and he eventually returned to his father with the Master's degree, and with Hanan.

The beauty and charm of Hanan won her not only the love and affection of her fiancé but also the welcome and acceptance of his family. So she ended up getting married and settling with her husband abroad, breaking away from her past and forgetting all the crises and disasters she has gone through, and among the things she forgot was me; her only brother left in the family! She traveled with her husband one year ago and I haven't heard from her since then, I don't even know where she lives and what she does.

As for me, I inherited the love of music from my mother, and just as painting and nervousness were my brother's inheritance from my father's side, music and calmness were my inheritance from my mother, and they were the only thing she had beside her exquisite beauty and her complete submission to my father. I fell in love with the piano from a very young age. My father tried to discourage me from playing the piano in favor of 'less expensive' instruments, but there was nothing else to satisfy my passion for music except the eighty-eight, black and white keys of this amazing instrument.

I struggled to learn piano, and I struggled to join the conservatoire, and I struggled to continue my studies there. My talent won me the approval of my teachers, but not their support, and my patience and perseverance got me their raised thumbs, but not their open arms. I was always the 'primo' among the students of the conservatoire, but the 'terso' when it comes to joining the conservatoire's teaching staff. I was on the honor's list but was never on the list of nominees for major performances, or to be one of the first-line players.

Indeed, to bequeath money without talent is glory with ignorance, but to bequeath talent without money is hell itself.

A gentle hand, that softly patted my shoulder, snatched me from the hole of my painful memories.

"Your music is great!"

I turned back to see who was talking, she was a woman in her late twenties, with short hair and a tinge of calm beauty, enhanced by her refined and elegant makeup, as well as her dress, whose delicateness was only overcome by its obvious priciness. I wondered who she was.

"I'm Dina," she replied to my wondering as if she'd read my thoughts! Now I must introduce myself in turn, how much I hate that!

"And you are Hamdi, a primo pianist, and one of Ihab's friends."

For the second time she'd read my thoughts! She excused me from introducing myself and did this part on my behalf.

"May I sit with you?"

I had this uneasy feeling when she asked to sit with me. I felt that I was going to regret that once day, but I answered her, "Help yourself."

"I am an artist like you, but I'm a fine artist; a sculptor to be precise. You play the notes and tackle the keys with your delicate fingers, but I caress the flint with my rough hands!"

She said that and gave a short laugh as she moved her fingers in front of my face. I smiled and did not answer. The first sign of lacking talent is a person claiming to have it! And here she was, starting her talk by saying, "I am an artist," which made me doubt that.

Dina started talking about herself, a quarter of an hour passed... half an hour... an hour... she was talking about herself without stopping. I wondered why she did that. Was it my silence and my quietness that left the control of any conversation to others? Or was it her mania and narcissism that were so obvious from the minute she started talking, and that pushed her to talk about herself and only about herself?

But what attracted me to keep listening to her was the names of her contacts! She kept mentioning the names of people that I have always dreamed of meeting one day, she kept mentioning them as if they were her relatives or close friends. She claimed to know Hans Mulland well; because her family was a big benefactor and supporter of his music school. She even claimed that she had a good relationship with Hans Zimmer! I always fantasized about meeting these people one day, and there she was telling me that they were all her close friends. This made me amused and eager to listen more to her... I'm the one who avoided talking to people and didn't answer the phone so as to keep it ringing with La Campanella and not to interrupt Lang Lang while he was playing!

That one-way chat ended an hour later, we exchanged our phone numbers with the promise to meet again next week to continue our 'conversation'.

I decided to leave, because I did not like this atmosphere of extravagance, nor could I afford it, so I quietly crossed the garden towards the gate, but I was surprised by Ihab calling me while walking quickly to catch me before I reached the gate.

"Are you leaving?!"

"Yes. Hans is gone, and I hope to hear from him soon, but now there's no need for me to stay. Thank you, Ihab. Thank you so much for all you've done for me. I really appreciate it."

Ihab smiled and shrugged his shoulders, saying, "I have done nothing for you, my friend, but rather have done Hans a favor. You are a talent that will add to his school's profile, but I don't think that he has much to add to your talent, he will only give you the name of his school as if it's a membership card to the great musicians club."

"We all need such an opportunity, my friend, and let Hans take from me what he wants to take. I don't care about anything as long as I join this great club, as you say."

"What do you think of her?"

Ihab surprised me with his question, so I turned to him and asked back, "Who?!"

Ihab smiled faintly and looked at me in a strange way, and said, "Dina... What do you think of her?"

I turned my face and looked far away to avoid looking at Ihab directly and said, "She's nice. She belongs more to your world than to mine, and she matches your whims more than she matches mine."

Ihab's face changed to become more serious, and he came closer to me, saying in a low voice.

"Listen, Hamdi. Dina is something else! She's something other than what you know about girls, she's really from another world. Dina belongs to one of the richest and most influential families in the country, they've reached such a degree of wealth and influence that you do not, and will not, hear about them. Look at all the luxury in which my family and I live, it is only because we pick up some crumbs that Dina's family throws carelessly to my father."

I was annoyed by what Ihab was saying, and I totally allowed my annoyance to show in the way I looked at him. I could not stand the rich people when they talked about themselves, especially when they complained and groaned about how 'poor' they were compared to their peers. So I answered Ihab in an angry voice, "And how does this concern me?"

Ihab took another step closer to me, and continued talking in a low voice. "Dina asked me about you. She wanted to know more about your life and your living, and she told me she would see you again next week. This means that she'll run a comprehensive and complete investigation about you and your family before she meets you..."

Ihab's words put me on fire, I hated it when people mentioned my family. So I interrupted him, defiantly, "Then tell her about me and my family, and you should warn her about me and my poverty, for I have nothing but talent and passion, other than that I have nothing..."

"No, my friend. I did not tell her anything, and I will not warn her about anyone. I am here to warn you!"

My anger from Ihab turned to surprise and astonishment. What was this strange thing he said? And what did he want to warn me about?

Ihab took two steps forward to stand exactly against me, he strongly grasped my elbows and said, "I've come to warn you about her! Dina is different. She's different from the rest of the people that you know. Her upbringing, her family, and the strength and influence that she has, all made her a different person who is difficult —or even impossible— to live with. She was married twice, and neither of the two marriages lasted more than six months. Young, rich and handsome men turned into ghosts after marrying her!"

I stared at Ihab, blank face. I could not understand what he was talking about. He continued to talk, "Hamdi. Listen carefully to what I have to say, and I will deny that I told you anything if I am ever asked about this discussion. I will even swear that you are a liar if you mention my name in connection with what we are talking about here ... Dina is a 'man eater'!! She chops men, grinds their flesh and crushes their bones without mercy or sympathy. Beware of her! Meet her cheerfully, talk to her gently and run away from her quickly. Say that you are traveling. Say that you are ill, even say that you are queer if you have to! But don't let her spin her web around you."

Dina

"A man bears who she is like me either to take advantage of her as a woman or to benefit from her as a tool, and here I am giving you a chance for both."

"Dina is a man-eater... She chops men... grinds their flesh and crushes their bones..."

Ihab's words were still ringing in my ears all day long. They we buzzing with sarcasm rather than fear. Poor Ihab! Do you really think that this Dina, the cute tiny creature, is a chopper?! Oh, Ihab! You should come to live my life so that you can know what the persecution of poverty and the oppression of men meant. Jobs I deserved but did not get, opportunities I desired but did not catch, and age that was advancing while I was not.

I forgot Ihab's words and went to meet Dina for the second time. It was only a few minutes that passed when Dina threw that question at me, "Tell me, Hamdi. What are your dreams?"

For the first time in our two meetings, Dina asked me a question about myself and showed interest in something other than her life.

"I hope to become a world-class pianist like Jan Lisiecki and Alexander Gadjiev. I hope I can become a Grandmaster pianist, and to have the opportunity to play the piano in the Opera of Vienna or the theaters of Paris. I want to play with the Berlin Philharmonic..."

"And what is stopping you?!"

Dina interrupted me with this question, which, to say the least, was the height of absurdity. But before I even started feeling annoyed, she, as usual and since I met her, excused me from making any effort to answer, as she preceded me in replying. She said, "Please. Don't throw at me words that lack any meaning and destroy every ambition; words that don't deserve to be added to language dictionaries, such as 'conditions', 'circumstances' and so forth. These words belong only to the arguments of disappointing slackers. I can't stand those words, nor those fools who lament about them, and I'm sure you're not one of those losers."

From that moment, Dina kept talking about resisting bad circumstances and not giving in to despair. Our meeting turned into one of these personal development classes that new university students get excited about, while those like me hate fiercely.

The only thing that forced me to listen to her without getting bored was the sheer amount of illustrious names that Dina mentioned during her hollow lecture; names that any single one of them was powerful and influential enough to introduce me to the world of art and music from the widest of its doors. Dina mentioned them one by one and told me about her 'personal' experience with them, and how they usually come to meet her and her family for advice and to ask for moral, and sometimes even financial, support.

The meeting was over and I went home with my head spinning like an amusement park wheel. I kept thinking of Dina, trying to figure out this extremely powerful yet incredibly annoying lady. Dina was like the lentil soup my mother used to make for us in the winter. It was nutritious and wholesome but tasted weird and was always very hot. It would burn my lips and inflame my tongue with my first sip from the dish. Would this 'dish' called Dina calm down and cool down with time? Or would it forever remain hot by the flames of its fiery ego?

I had numerous meetings with Dina since then, although they were all quick meetings and never exceeded an hour. I was busy with my life and she was busy with hers; her life that despite her talking about it for hours and hours I didn't really know anything about! Dina talked a lot but she didn't say anything. She mentioned details of events and names of people, but didn't reveal emotions or express feelings. She spoke about herself like a public relations manager talking about her company, not like a person talking about his life. I knew a lot about her power and influence, but I didn't know anything about herself except that she talked about this 'self' to the point of obsession; an obsession with the appearance that had nothing to do with the essence. The hot soup hadn't cooled down, it was still burning my mouth, and I still didn't like its taste.

* * * *

"I will marry you!"

Dina said that, as she put the straw in her mouth and started drinking her juice without looking at me. I was not only surprised by what she said, I was also surprised by how indifferent she sounded. This was our fifth meeting, and we were not at that time talking about anything related to, or that even carried a hint of affection or acceptance, but she said this word without fear or hesitation.

"Won't you give me a chance to think about your proposal first?"

I threw my sarcastic question with a smile in an attempt to turn the subject into a joke, because that was what I thought it was, but Dina replied to me with all seriousness, and said, "You thought about it! I could even say that you planned it, but you are too shy to take the first step. We have been meeting for more than a month, I do nothing but speak about myself and you do nothing but listen. I didn't give you a single chance to speak about yourself, and you didn't ask for it. This is what a man does with a woman when he looks beyond friendship.

A man bears who she is like me either to take advantage of her as a woman or to benefit from her as a tool, and here I am giving you a chance for both."

I was astonished. Dina's frankness always managed to amaze me, and her bluntness never failed to stun me, but this time her frankness was so crude to the point of harshness. Ladies these days do not know how much their beauty diminishes the franker they are, nor do they know how less attractive a woman can be the more vulgar she becomes.

But, as usual, Dina didn't give me the chance to think or to reflect.

"Listen, Hamdi. Let me shorten the distances between us, and this is what I am good at while those like you are not. I see what I want, and I go to it and get it. As for people like you, half of their lives are wasted in anticipation and wishful thinking, then the other half is wasted in regret for what they missed thinking and anticipating."

Dina's bluntness that always amounted to rudeness never seized to surprise me since I knew her. My eyes were getting wider and wider as she continued talking, "Listen, I'm a friendless person! I have thousands and thousands of acquaintances and relationships, but I don't have a single friend. Do you know why?! Because friendship is based on the exchange of feelings, and I don't have feelings to exchange with anyone else! Also, friendship is based on sharing my life with others, and I am selfish, egoistic. I don't like to share any of my things with others, even if it's a piece of bread, so how about my life?!"

I was astonished by her words that absolutely crippled my tongue. It was rare for a narcissist to admit their narcissism in that way. Usually, such a confession would come from those who responded to psychotherapy, or from those whose narcissism had ended in complete madness. To which group did you belong, Dina?!

As usual, Dina did not give me any time to continue my thoughts. She gazed at me with her penetrating looks and said, "I will marry you. You will bear with my selfishness and ego, and I will open the gates of glory to you. I will not give you money, nor will I recommend you to any of my acquaintances, but I will put you in the same room with all the emperors of music you wish to meet and dream about talking to.

I'll have you play in front of them all the beautiful sonatas and concertos you love and master, and the rest is up to you and your talented fingers. I am nothing but the gate, logging in is your job."

Dina finished her words and then got up to leave, she said while picking up her small bag, "I'll be waiting for a call from you tomorrow at this time; a call telling me that you agree to the marriage. If you have a different opinion, don't call. Don't bother to apologize, just don't call tomorrow... and don't call ever again!"

Speechless, Dina left me and left the place. I didn't know what to do or what to say. By any calculation, this was the opportunity of a lifetime. It was the ladder for glory and the paved way to the laurels of music; the world that I have always panted running behind and which has always evaded me. This world would come to me through Dina's gate and in Dina's bed, it would ask, or even beg me to go through it to take my well-deserved place among great musicians, and then I won't need a membership card from Hans to get into the club of great musicians, because I'm going to be on the board of this club!

However, the price seemed to be heavy, Dina... What a price! Meeting her once a week was a challenge to my endurance, so what about living with her every single day?!

And what about what Ihab said to me?! Dina, the mincer, the man-eater. Should I go back and talk to him? Perhaps then he would tell me more about the reasons for his concerns? Ihab has always been good to me, but he also has always kept it to himself. He had the heart of a passionate musician but the mind of a sneaky businessman, hiding more than he was showing. He would never share the details of his inner circle with someone like me. The greatest example of this was Hans' visit; Ihab put me in the same room with him, and arranged for him to listen to me playing, but how? And why? He did not and would not tell me.

Therefore, his rushing behind me that night only to warn me of Dina, and his suspicious and strange way of talking about her suggested that there were many secrets about which I did not know anything, so should I leave what's hidden as is? Or should I try to reveal what might disturb my decision and take me away from the road to glory?

I got to my house. I didn't know how I got there and which way I took, I was totally lost in thoughts and wandering through speculations. I lay on my bed fully clothed and fully cluttered; I found my mind leading me to think about the past, the past that I've been trying to forget.

My father refused my mother's work in the field of music that she loved and mastered, under the pretext of traditions and conventionalism. He stopped her from accepting good jobs that would save us from poverty, even her work in the field of teaching was rejected by 'his majesty'. He sacrificed any opportunity for additional income to satisfy his pride and arrogance. He wanted to be the only provider for this family and therefore be the only ruler in the house. In the end, my mother surrendered to his tyranny, and he surrendered to his poverty, and poverty became the one and only ruler in this miserable house. My brother refused to sell his works for huge sums of money under the pretext of talent and the rights of the artist, so he ended up drenched in his blood in the bathroom that became his altar and his slaughterhouse.

My sister was the only sane one, she was the one who used her mind and thought her life through, she cared about her sanity and ignored her spontaneity, unleashed her ambition and curbed her passion, and there she was living a good life that had no place in it for me.

As for me, my situation was different. I was not selling my talent or giving up my art. On the contrary, I was striving to achieve my dream, earn my glory, and make my way. I didn't bury my dreams or neglect them, but I revived and resurrected them.

And if that required me to struggle and toil in front of the piano and also in bed. Why not?! It was the sedulity and perseverance I would exert to reach my ultimate goal.

At this point, I fell asleep...

Ashraf Ibrahim

The Proposal

"When others refuse to receive our calls, we find ourselves rushing to answer any call incoming, even if it is a call from a creditor. It is the human soul that cannot tolerate rejection."

In the morning I was at the peak of vigilance and vigor. I made up my mind and made my decision. Let Dina be my gateway to the world of glory, and let Ihab, his fears, and his Fazioli all go to hell!

It was ten in the morning, and there was still time before my call with Dina, but I decided to call her right away, as if my mind wanted to cut my line of return. I called her; the phone rang once; she cancelled the call! Then a short message came to me, "Call me on time!"

Oh Dina! Please don't make this harder than it already is. Narcissism and ego are fatal to any relationship, but one can be wise enough to come to terms with them. However, when rudeness is added to the mix, the result is capable of destroying any kind of understanding or compromise.

I decided at that time to call Ihab, I needed to tell him about what happened, and what would happen between Dina and I, at least out of courtesy and good manners. I was sure it would come as a surprise to him, and he would try to dissuade me from this decision with all his might, but I was determined to go ahead with that marriage, and I would not let him be in my way to glory.

I called him... He, too, hung up. Showers of questions started flooding my brain, 'What is happening today? Is Ihab avoiding me? And why? Has he received any bad news from Hans? Or does he know about Dina and I? Did Dina tell him? What will he do to stop me?'

Only a minute passed and I found my phone ringing, an unknown number. I didn't leave the opportunity for Lang Lang to play 'La Campanella', I answered quickly. When others refuse to receive our calls, we find ourselves rushing to answer any call incoming, even if it is a call from a creditor. It is the human soul that cannot tolerate rejection.

The caller was Ihab.

"Eh, Ihab? What is this strange number? What happened to the old one?"

"Hamdi, my dear friend. I am so sorry I didn't take your call. Just know that from now on if you try to call me I will not answer, but will call you afterward from another number like I'm doing now."

I was surprised by Ihab's strange talk. I considered his words a kind of ridiculous joke that deserved a ridiculous response, so I replied to him saying, "Why this vibe of mystery? Did you apply for a job in intell..."

Ihab interrupted me before I could finish the joke, telling me in all seriousness. "Hamdi, listen, my friend. I know that you meet Dina regularly. I know that you are drawn to her world as a butterfly is attracted to light, and I am sure that you intend to propose to her or she is the one who intends to propose to you! In both cases, you and she will get married! You will weaken in front of her luster and brightness, and accept marriage to her and perhaps even seek it, and then our relationship as friends will be over. In fact, we might not see each other for a long time."

"Why all this, my friend? Were you planning to propose to her?"

Ihab answered my question with a screeching laugh, then he said in a voice that combined laughter and sorrow,

"Oh, Hamdi. If everything went well and we met again, I might then have the courage to tell you more about my reasons. Let's finish this call now. And remember, my friend. I warned you about the man-eater!"

Ihab ended the phone call after he poured a million gallons of cold water on my enthusiasm. The biggest enemy of ambition is not drugs; it's confusion. For a person to receive a warning supported with reasons, this is a call to reflection and precaution. As for receiving a warning without reason, this is a call for endless confusion and disabling doubt.

Time passed by between Dina's glamorous promises pulling my mind towards her and Ihab's mysterious warnings pushing me away. Finally, the moment came, it was the time for my call with Dina. It was in vain to expect her to return my earlier call. So I grabbed my phone and looked at her number before I dared to hit the call button.

"Hello. How are you, Dina?"

That lunatic didn't even give me a chance to talk, she didn't even return the greeting, "I usually don't give others a chance to reconsider their options, but I know this is a big decision for you to make, so I will ask you one last time. Have you made up your mind?"

"Dina, you are talking to me as if you are buying a car! This is marriage, engagement, and..."

"No, sir. I'm not buying a car. I'm buying a man!"

Dina said it while laughing as if she liked the joke she made. Although the 'buy a man' banter was accepted among people, it hit me like a heavy stone perching on my chest. Why didn't I accept her joke? Was it because of Dina's way that was devoid of taste? Or because it was the truth? She was, actually, buying a man!

It was time to meet Dina's parents, and as our 'marriage proposal' was awkward and strange, so was the way I met her parents. I didn't ask for them to bless our marriage in a private, close family gathering as usual, but I met them at a party they held in one of the palaces they own. Despite the oddity of the way and form this meeting was planned, I was happy with it. The traditional way of asking for the bride's hand required me to bring my family or my close relatives, and I had neither.

Dina's dad met me at the party in a summery linen shirt and sandals, while I was wearing a full suit and a tie. I was fully formal, and he was entirely casual.

Fortunately, he didn't give me enough time to compare our attire, "Your name is Hamdi, right?"

"Yes, sir. I am Hamdi."

"Do you want to marry Dina?"

"It is my honor, sir."

"May God be with you!"

I did not have any time to reply, or even to say Amen to his prayer. The man threw that strange answer at me and then went away, he did not ask me about anything or ask me for anything, he did not try to get to know me or even get the basic information about me, I had the approval of one of the most powerful men in the country to marry his only daughter in less than a minute!

Perhaps the man was busy with what was more important, he might leave such matters to his wife to organize and manage such family ceremonies. I looked around, searching for Dina, I found her standing away with a group of people. She waved to me and smiled; she then looked the other side to whisper in the ear of an elegant lady standing beside her. The lady was so classy and graceful although she was wearing a simple summery linen outfit like the one Dina's father was wearing. Perhaps it was the elegant accessories she was wearing or the aristocratic look she enjoyed. I found her waving to me while smiling. She was definitely Dina's mother; the similarity was clear and unmistakable, and the Linen outfit confirmed her connection with Dina's father. I love those women who manage to create glamour and flair around themselves with the simplest and most natural accessories.

But my admiration to the lady vanished quickly, thanks to my anxiety. The situation was all new to me so I felt embarrassed and confused. Should I go and meet Dina's mother and get to know her? Or should I wait until she leaves the group she was with and comes to me? She pointed at me with a smile and then got back to her party. Were they talking about me? Or would she not even bother to talk with me or about me?!

Suddenly I found Dina holding my arm. I didn't notice that she left her mother's group and walked towards me. I was immersed in thinking about Dina's parents, and comparing them to mine. My mother is definitely more beautiful than her mother, and her father is definitely more intelligent than my father.

"Huh. is the interview over?"

Dina said that while smiling, she was referring to my 'meeting' with her father. If I can call this half-a-minute chat a meeting!

"Or has it even started?! Your father gave me less than a minute of his precious time, then off he went."

I replied to Dina and smiled sarcastically. She gave me the same sarcastic smile and said, "This is our world, Hamdi. Everyone gets what he wants and does not waste his time in pointless and meaningless formalities. Come with me. I want to introduce you to our guests."

Dina started introducing me to her guests ... Hamdi, Pianist Primo, Ramzi Yassa of the future, the next Andsnes! Dina gave me all the titles and granted me all the conceivable qualities that could be given to a great musician, but not once did she introduce me as her fiancé.

The next day, Dina invited me to a new party. This time it was not a family party, but a party with many of her acquaintances. At this party I found a Bogányi piano resting in the middle of the hall. However, among the guests there were no musicians, no singers, and there was nothing musical about the guests. So both the Bogányi and I seemed like intruders to this party which did not need such a grand piano or such a desperate pianist.

Dina asked me to play, and I started playing some famous pieces that such audiences might like. I played 'Für Elise' by Beethoven, 'Turkish March' by Mozart, and 'Winter' from 'The Four Seasons' by Vivaldi. All are great music , and all may be familiar, or at least palatable, to those audience

The party continued until the early hours of the morning, and so did the other parties that continued every day, without interruption. Every day there was a new party and a new occasion; a birthday, a family event, a work party, a gathering of sculptors, the weekly artist meeting.

Bogányi Piano

There was always a reason and there was always a party! And at every party I found my friend, the Bogányi, lying in the middle of the hall... an outsider like me, a stranger to this world that hosted music without tasting it.

A month passed like a long and tiring day. My tiredness and my continuous lack of sleep compelled me to withdraw from all the work I used to do in the morning, and my evening engagements with Dina and her parties forced me to quit all the work I was doing in the evening.

The only time I had to myself was in the afternoon, between three and eight. That was the only time I could work for my living, but what job could a pianist like myself have and at the same time fit these afternoon hours? It was the piano lessons.

| **Turkish March** | **Für Elise** | **Winter** |
| Mozart | Beethoven | Vivaldi |

Teaching piano was the only job that could be done at that time, the only job that didn't require much effort from my side, the only job that guaranteed me a good steady income, and the only job that I hated in my life! I hated piano lessons as much as I hated death.

Imagine that you waste hours and hours explaining the basics of the eighty-eight keys that you spent your life addressing and accosting, while those calling themselves 'students' did not understand anything about them and could not see any difference between them! What was required from you as a piano tutor was to teach them the difference between each key and the other, then teach them how to differentiate between various sounds and melodies, then how to move between these keys in all the softness and lightness, then how to produce notes that corresponded to melodies and could be classified as music, then how to add from his feeling and sense to this melody, then ... then ... It's hell! Especially when fate afflicted you with those who did not have the delicate sense or the musical ear, yet they were determined to learn to play the piano out of social prestige. These people were usually the most generous spenders on piano lessons but benefited the least from these lessons. These people were the fantasy of all con artists claiming to be music instructors, and the nightmare of every talented musician who venerated and revered their art.

In secrecy, I started the piano lessons, I did not tell Dina anything about them, I was afraid that my interest in teaching piano would reveal my scarce finances and my need for money. Of course, I was not going against Dina and her family, and all the piano lessons in the world would never put me in any material comparison with them, but at least I would be able to cover my own expenses. I deliberately chose the affluent families, but I avoided the very wealthy ones so that I would not meet anyone who might know me or Dina.

The lessons began, and so did the chronic headaches and the constant exhaustion. A talented musician is like a free bird; trapping it in a cage kills it and eliminates its talent. And there is no narrower cage or tighter imprisonment than piano lessons. It destroys any creativity remaining in me and drains any passion remaining inside my veins. For me, nothing kills creativity like captivity.

Nevertheless, I continued serving my sentence! I had to secure a source of income to live from so I could keep up with Dina in her never-drying parties.

The parties continued and so did the piano lessons. I began to feel bored, or even nauseous, from Dina's endless and useless activities; I hated talking to people without prior knowledge and without later benefit. I was still meeting new people, but none of them could be of benefit to my career, and I was still hearing the words of praise and admiration, but none of them was followed by discussing the next step in my future. I was still Hamdi ... Pianist Primo ... the next Andsnes ... and that was it. Dina kept hiding the fact that I was her fiancé, and I kept hiding the fact that I was a music teacher.

* * * *

"The wedding will be next week."

Dina threw the word into my ears while checking her mobile as if it were a passing sentence. but frankly I was not surprised by what she said. As a matter of fact, I was expecting her to do so. A woman with such controlling behavior would definitely set the date and the details of her marriage on her own. Let's not forget that she was the one who proposed to me! As for myself, I knew that my role in this relationship would be limited to listening and obeying. However, I felt it was a good opportunity to vent my anger and frustration with her arrogance and her dominating behavior, so I decided to evade her and to coquet like little girls, "Which wedding, Dina?!"

"Our wedding... you and me."

"Dina. If you don't give me enough respect as your fiancé and future husband, at least give me my respect as a man!"

She moved her eyes away from her mobile only to give me one of her frigid looks, as she said softly, "What do you want?"

"Dina, we need to settle these matters together; we might discuss and argue, or even fight, but in the end, our decision needs to be a joint one that we both are satisfied with."

Dina's looks turned from the icy blank to one full of sarcasm and mockery. She then said, "What, Hamdi? Are you busy next week? Can't you postpone your piano lessons even for one day?"

Dina's words petrified me... She knew! I tried to hide my piano lessons as much as I could, but all my attempts were in vain... She knew!

"Let the wedding be on Tuesday. Ramy's lesson ends at five, which gives you time to get ready. Is this Okay, Hamdi?"

The witch! Not only did she know about my piano lessons, she even knew the names of my clients! The mysterious words of Ihab jumped to my head, Dina knows everything! She knew all about me and about my past, present and possibly future life. She proved that Ihab was right by saying, "Listen, Hamdi. You are free to tell me what you want to tell or to hide what you want to hide. I won't get angry with you, and I won't blame you, because I honestly don't care. Just remember one thing; I know everything about you. Let the wedding be on Tuesday after Ramy's lesson. I will send you the address. The party will be casual attire, so don't bring a suit and a tie!"

Getting up from her seat to announce the end of that awkward meeting, and before she went away, Dina looked at me and said with a smile, "The beautiful thing, Hamdi, is that you have no family to bear their concern, so I don't need to tell you that, from your side, you are the only one invited to this wedding."

At that moment I began to seriously think about

running away from Dina and the whole idea of marrying her. That woman scared me! I felt like she was an evil goddess in Greek mythology; she knew what no one could know and acted as she pleased without anyone's permission, and I neither could nor desired to marry Greek evil Gods. Plus, she called me the 'invited'! Have you seen someone being 'invited' to his own wedding?!

However, there was nothing I could do. The days were passing by and I had not heard any news from Hans, and here was my relationship with music getting cut off after I left everything to keep up with Dina in her busy schedule, and my relationship with the piano has become limited to my daily training and my miserable lessons. Dina was the best path to glory, now she was the only way to it.

The voice of my impudent greed triumphed over the sound of my justified fears, so I decided to go through with that marriage knowing that it was doomed to failure. All I was hoping for was for it not to fail before I reaped the benefits of its connections and access to the world of professional musicians and international   concerts.

The Marriage

"Why did Dina's call make me so terrified? Is it my fear of her that she instilled in my heart from the first day I met her? Or is it my ear, which was so skilled at appreciating and evaluating sounds, that it was able to discern the danger and pick it up clearly from her voice over the phone?"

It's Monday. I decided to spend the morning arranging for the next 'big' day. I discovered that I did not discuss with Dina where we would live after marriage! After some thoughts, I decided to call her, and to bring up the topic in a light and peppy way,

"Could Your Majesty be sympathetic and gracious, and tell me where we shall live after marriage? Of course, I would love to have you living with me in my modest apartment, though I think it is much more inferior than the bottom of your expectations."

Dina laughed uproariously as she said, "No, sir. You are invited to live with me in my villa, not because I am above living in your apartment, but because the workshop where I work on my sculptures is there, which makes life a lot easier for me. I got a new piano for you on the third floor of the villa. This floor will be a hermitage for you and for your music, while the first floor will be for me and my sculptures."

I took advantage of the serenity and tranquillity of her mood, so I said to her in a low voice, "And what about the second floor?"

Dina gave me another laugh, but one with a lot of debaucheries and a little fun, and said,

"This is your floor, and this is your role; your role is to make me fall in love with you, and to show me what kind of a man you are. And beware of me! Just as I am a hard-to-please woman in life, I am a very picky woman in love. I will have my requests and demands that you must honor and obey. I expect you to understand me as a woman and to respect me as the woman, and if you did so you will find your way to heaven... through me."

At this point the call ended, Dina ended it and left me feeling the fire of confusion consuming my mind. Why did Dina's call make me so terrified? Is it my fear of her that she instilled in my heart from the first day I met her? Or is it my ear, which was so skilled at appreciating and evaluating sounds, that it was able to discern the danger and pick it up clearly from her voice over the phone?

Finally, it was Tuesday. I couldn't get much sleep, so I woke up early but lounged in bed until noon. I went to deliver my piano lesson, as Dina had told me, and then went home to get ready for the wedding.

Once I opened the door and walked into my house, I remembered my family... I remembered my father, my mother, Hanan... and Hassan. I imagined if they were with me today. My mother watching me with her beautiful eyes that show how happy she is that her firstborn son is getting married. My father looking at me proudly and happily while keeping his serious features and his always frowning forehead. Hanan running to her room to bring me the wedding suit and bragging about the effort she made in preparing it. Hassan pushing me jokingly and asking me if I am ready for tonight's 'battle', and my father rebukes him and forbids him to talk barefaced in front of my sister... Everyone is laughing... Everyone is happy... Everyone is a ghost!

Wake up, Hamdi! All of those you dream about are gone forever. They ran away and abandoned you, leaving you to beg for glory from the gates of Dina. So don't shed tears over their loss and don't light candles to their souls, as they are the cause of your misery in this world.

I put on my wedding outfit according to Dina's orders, a light set of Linen like the ones her parents wore at the party, and I put on light shoes. I was going to wear sandals, but I felt that would be too casual. With Dina, one should strictly follow her precise orders.

The wedding party started at nine, and was over by eleven! A party where there was nothing to indicate that it was a wedding. Even the invitees were inferior to Dina's smallest parties. Most of them were bohemian sculptors who aimlessly wander in the arms of the stone idols they make by their own hands.

We headed home; I mean Dina's house. It was a very elegant and simple villa; small in its size, great in its splendor. Dina grabbed my arm and took me straight to the third floor to show me my 'music hermitage' as she called it. It was indeed a masterpiece; the Steinway piano in the middle of the hall, the pictures of many great musicians adorned the walls. Among those pictures, there were three frames with musical notes inside. I was drawn to these musical notes hanging in the frames and shining thanks to the copper-coated spotlights spotted on them. I approached those frames with Dina still clasping my arm and explaining to me what was in them,

"'Philip the Wanderer'... original note... signed by Cassandra Miller."

"Wow! How did you get it?!"

"And this is 'where cobalt wave'... an original... dedicated to you personally by Ann Cleare."

"Ann Cleare herself?!"

"This is the 'Water in the Glass' musical notes... by Natalie Dreyer."

I didn't know what to say, this woman knew how to take me by surprise. These were all music sheets dedicated to my name by some of the greatest contemporary musicians and piano composers! Some are signed by those great musicians themselves, and some are the originals of their work!

Finally, I turned to Dina in amazement and said, "Looks like you paid a big amount of money to get these notes!"

Dina looked at me with stagy anger tinged with a malicious laugh and said in fondness, "Don't say a big amount of money, say a small fortune!"

Her reply embarrassed me. I, who came to the

wedding empty-handed, and didn't even bring a bouquet of roses. I tried to change the subject, keeping it away from money, "But I noticed that they were all ladies; Cassandra, Anne Cleare, Natalie."

Dina continued her pampering and malicious smile and said, "Yes, I did it on purpose. So that they would keep their eyes on you all the time, and keep me informed of what you do, day and night."

I looked at her with lust more than love. "You don't need them to keep an eye on me. From today onwards, I'm all yours."

It was our first night together as husband and wife. Our relationship was more objective and planned than spontaneous and emotional. Dina dictated her orders and I had to obey her. There was a great deal of orders and instructions from Dina's side, there was obedience and submission from my side, and there was no love at all from either sides. I felt like we were a manager and a subordinate working in an office and not a married couple in their first night as a husband and wife.

The night passed with its passions and its directions. It was only an hour until I was falling into a deep sleep, from which I did not wake up until the early morning hours. I slept happily and ecstatically, for being able to obey Dina's commands and doing exactly what was asked of me. I always believed that virility is to rejoice in your victory in the battlefield of bed, while wisdom is to rejoice in the victory of your opponent, and I was a wise man, my happiness lay in the happiness of my opponent—I meant my wife.

Suddenly I remembered her... my wife... Dina. I didn't find her beside me in bed or in the room. I got out of bed to look for her, but I couldn't find her anywhere. After a few minutes, I heard continuous knocking coming from the first floor, I got dressed and went down to the workshop. I knocked on the door, Dina opened it; she opened a slit so narrow that I could only see half of her face.

"Yes."

I was astonished by her strange response and the gelid look she threw at me, "Dina! What are you doing so early?"

"Working, as you can see."

"Now, Dina?! On our first morning together?! On the first day of what is supposed to be our honeymoon?"

"It is the inspiration, Hamdi ... the inspiration. It comes without an appointment and respects no schedules, and it came to me this morning, so I hurried down to my workshop to capture it before it ran away. Don't worry, it won't be long. I'll finish in a little while, and then I'll come up to you."

"But can't this inspiration wait until we have breakfast?"

I said it jokingly, but she didn't take my joke very well, "This is something you will never understand, Hamdi, because you are just a musician trying to catch the inspirations that afflicted others and follow them. You do not produce anything from scratch and do not create anything new. You only excel in imitating the original creators! As for me, I only do what my inspiration dictates. I do not imitate anyone's creation and do not follow in anyone's footsteps. I have nothing but my inspiration to follow."

It was time for me to get back upstairs. I heard enough insults and had enough humiliation for one morning, so I collected my scattered dignity and ascended to the second floor while talking to myself ... Dina, How mean you are!

Yesterday you were introducing me to your acquaintances as the next music prodigy, and today you tell me that I'm like a monkey imitating those around me without real talent. Yesterday in front of the piano I was a monster, today I am a monkey?!

Radi

"When I grew up I learned that the wicked hid behind the habits and moves of the honest and took them as a cover for their evil intentions, and that a hand on the chest did not necessarily mean kindness."

There is nothing to help washing out one's insults like a good cup of coffee, so I made myself one and then headed to the balcony. It was a beautiful morning and the air was fresh and cool, which helped me swallow Dina's insult and return to the happy and clear state I felt when I woke up.

From the balcony, I saw a man actively and diligently washing Dina's car. He was a dark man in his late sixties, of a poor build and a wrinkled face that glowed with the kindness of the heart and serenity of the spirit. His face reminded me of my brother Hassan's when he had finished working on one of his paintings, the same calm and contentment that radiated from his face after days and nights of revolt and madness.

The man saw me watching him from the balcony so he quickly raised his hand to salute me.

I greeted him with a nod as he lowered his hand and placed it on his chest and then continued to wash the car.

My mother used to do the same move; she also used to put her hand on her chest after greeting anyone. She always insisted that those who did that move were kind-hearted. She believed that the 'good people' who greet sincerely put their hands on their chests after the salutation, but the 'bad guys' did not bother to do so. When I grew up I learned that the wicked hid behind the habits and moves of the honest and took them as a cover for their evil intentions, and that a hand on the chest did not necessarily mean kindness. However, I could see that this person already carried all the signs of pure goodness.

A few moments later, a young man appeared walking with faltering steps and heading towards the old man. The young man started talking nervously while the old man was trying to calm him down, the voice of the young man rose so the old man tried to put his hand on his mouth to silence him, the young man revolted and pushed him so he fell to the ground.

I never got myself involved in situations like this and didn't like to be a part of any quarrel or even an argument, so I chose to keep quiet and watch what was happening. Suddenly, Dina entered the balcony, looked at me with a doubtful smile and said, "What are you doing?"

"I was enjoying my coffee till I saw this. That young man seems to be assaulting the old fellow."

Dina looked at me slyly and said, "Shouldn't you go and help him? He needs a strong man like you to defend him."

I grabbed her hand and kissed it while saying, "My dear. I have enough battles with my future and my music. I do not have the power or the desire to interfere in the affairs of others, even if it is for the sake of fairness and justice. Also, these fingers were not created for hitting and fighting, but for playing the piano."

At that moment, I was expecting her to exchange some intimacy or even a little pampering, for today is our first day as a married couple, but she gave me a long look, then said.

"Get ready to go out, we are invited to lunch."

Invitation for lunch on the morning of our wedding?! Shouldn't we have our own time together? Even for a day or two? That's what I was asking myself.

But frankly, it didn't matter to me as long as it made her happy. I finished my shower and quickly got dressed. Dina needed an hour to be ready, so I made myself another cup of coffee and went to the balcony, but the good weather and the warm sun tempted me to pay a visit to the little garden. I grabbed a small chair and sat down, took out my headphones and started sipping my coffee and enjoying my favorite music. How I wished my life was as calm and soft as the sun of that day, but that was something only simple people with simple lives could enjoy.

I've always thought that talent is a curse, and the greater it was, the more it overwhelmed the mind of its owner and eroded his happiness. All the great musicians lived a life of misery and anguish thanks to the presence of their talent and the absence of their common sense... Mozart, Beethoven, Mahler,

---

Mozart K.488 Piano Concerto #23 in A 2nd mov. Adagio

Rachmaninoff, Van Gogh, Georgia O'Keeffe, Jimi Hendrix, Karen Carpenter, a long list of musicians, painters, writers, poets and singers... differed in their talents and art, and met in their misery and torment. Talent is like a medicine, a little of it is a cure while a lot of it is a poison.

I turned to my right and found the old man, whom I had seen in the morning, standing at a distance as if he was waiting for permission to approach me. I took off the headphones and smiled at him. The man approached timidly and stood not a short distance from me and then said in a calm voice, "Good morning, sir, I am Radi. Your servant Radi, the keeper of this villa. If you have any requests, please ask me and I will do them immediately, and when your car arrives, please let me know so I can wash it for you daily. And congratulations, sir."

"Thank you, Radi. You are a good man. Where are you from, Radi?"

"From the south, sir."

"I am also from the south, although I've never been there in my life, but my father was pure southern, like you, Radi."

"God forbid it, sir. Your father must've come from better origins than mine."

I looked at Radi and smiled. I was sure he made more money from his housekeeping and car washing than my father's salary when he was an art teacher.

As for the origin, I could guess that my grandfather and Radi's father were both working as slaves in the same land owned by one of the old landlords in the nineteen-twenties, and that they were both flogged with the same whip when they were lazy at work.

"Who is this young man who was arguing with you a while ago?"

I wasn't sure why I asked Radi about this, but I felt that I wanted to know more. Radi flinched as if he didn't want me to know who this young man was, or that he didn't like to talk about him, but he came back to say, "He is my son, Sayed. He is a good and decent young man, but he is mentally ill. May God heal his soul."

I shook my head and smiled.

At that moment Dina appeared at the door, and as soon as Radi saw her, he hurried out of the garden as if he didn't want her to see him talking to me.

We set off in the car. Dina was driving silently while I was listening to music. I tried to break the strange silence imposed by this moody lunatic that

I took for a wife, "Poor Sayed. He seems to be causing his father so much torment."

Dina furrowed her eyebrows in surprise and said, "Sayed who?!"

"The son of Radi, the guard of the villa. His mental illness seems to overshadow his relationship with his father."

Dina smiled sarcastically and glanced at me, then looked back at the road and said, "Mental illness?! What mental illness, you gullible?! He is a heroin addict!"

"Oh really?! I didn't notice that, although I know addicts and what they look like. Maybe it was the distance that prevented me from seeing that he's an addict."

"He is a disturbed young man. Had my father not loved Radi so much, we would have had another way to deal with him and his son. But my father insists on keeping Radi in my service, and with him comes this fool, Sayed. It's like a buy one get one free offer."

Dina said the last sentence and smiled sarcastically.

I preferred silence, so I did not comment on what she said. Dina kept driving and I kept my mouth shut until we arrived at where we were going. The day passed lingeringly having lunch with Dina's acquaintances, useless conversations, fake smiles, and time moving like a turtle.

* * * *

Nights and nights rolled by, and every evening I found a piano waiting for me to fulfill the requests of those present and gain their blessings, and every night I found a house waiting for me to fulfill Dina's commands and obtain her blessings.

These boring, useless and humiliating evenings started to make me more and more nauseous; they were a waste of time, just as Dina's companion has become a waste of dignity. All her invited guests were Bohemian sculptors and painters ... No musicians, no music, and no glory. None of the attendees had any influence, handling, or even understanding of the world of classical music, nor of the glorious world of piano.

Even Dina's way of introducing me has changed. I was no longer Hamdi the Primo pianist, and I was no longer the next Andsnes. I just became Hamdi who played piano upon request!

Parent executorily

One night, and after an exhausting evening, I decided to bring up my concerns to her.

"Dina, please don't get me wrong, but in all these evenings and parties we attend I find no one who can help me enter the world of music in the way I desire."

"Hamdi. Don't be a child! Things like this require time and planning. I cannot invite my acquaintances who have the keys for your world of music to hear my husband playing. It should come naturally as if it were a coincidence. They need to hear about you and about how people admire your skills before they can hear you and listen to you playing. It is that aura of fame and admiration that will make them more accepting of you and ready to help you."

"But—"

"Listen, my love. You plan one step ahead, while I plan several steps further. I'm planning for Paris, Vienna and Broadway. So let me plan for you, wisely and quietly, and do not rush me."

I withdrew back to my silence, not convinced by any of what she just said. Her answers made me more worried about my career and less trusting of her promises. I ended up wondering what this witch was up to.

Dina suddenly decided to 'relieve' me from her parties. She started spending more time in her workshop, claiming that she was committed to an exhibition that she would open in two months, and that she had to finish all the work she had already started. She also began to attend many parties without me, holding me to my argument about the uselessness of these parties for my future. So she decided to make me attend only the ones that she believed to be beneficial to me and my career. As for the rest, she started attending them alone.

My life was misery, but it was an organised misery. I would get up late and spend the rest of the morning practicing piano, then I would head to my students for their piano lessons. Despite my hatred for it, I began to use it as an escape from the villa, so I accepted a number of new students, and I worked from two in the afternoon until eight in the evening, then I got back to my piano practicing. The third floor became a true hermitage for my music, and I became the devoted monk on the altar of music; a monk with only one sin, Dina.

Sayed

"The basis of recovery from addiction is the sincere and strong desire of addicts to be cured. As for Sayed, he had a sincere and strong desire to die."

It was another lonely and boring evening when I was surprised by a knock on the door. That was not Radi's. I had known Radi's way of knocking by then. Who would it be? and how did this person manage to reach the third floor without permission? I cautiously opened the door only to find Sayed, the addict son of Radi, standing there. He was smiling foolishly with shaky lips, and staring at me with these peevish looks coming out from his bloody red eyes. After a moment of awkward silence, he mumbled,

"I want money... any money... please."

I was about to dismiss him and shut the door, but he put his hand inside to prevent me from closing it, then continued mumbling desperately, "Please... listen... you are stronger than me... you can push me out and even hit me... or close the door and crush my hand... and I'm a poor thing that can do nil... all I want is a little money... please!"

 89

I don't know what made me do what I did, but I put my hand into my pocket, took out all the money I had there, and gave it to Sayed.

As soon as this poor young man saw the money, his eyes bulged and he started drooling. He snatched it from my hand and ran like crazy. I closed the door and lamented the circumstances of this lost soul. I tried to forget this incident and to get back to my piano, but only to find new knockings on the door. Was this wanderer back again?

I opened the door slightly and deliberately put my foot behind the door to prevent Sayed from pushing it if his addiction had made him more reckless. But it was not him; it was his father, Radi, standing far away and looking at me shyly,

"I'm so sorry, sir. Oh my God, I'm so sorry... Did... Did Sayed come here?"

"Yes, Radi. Sayed came here to ask for money, and I gave him some. All is well. He appears to be a good young man, but life has taken him for the worse."

"I'm sorry, sir... I'm very sorry... He... He is a good boy... but... but... May God help him."

The man burst into tears; he was definitely about to collapse. I tried to calm him down by saying, "Do not despair, Radi. It's nothing but a whim, and after that, he will return to the right path."

With mumbles that were worse than his son's, Radi collected his broken nerves and scattered tears and left, and I went back to the piano, trying to get all that happened out of my mind. I already had my own misery and my own dilemma. I didn't think the problems of others would cheer me up.

Two hours later, there was a new knock on the door. It was Sayed again, but that time he seemed calm and subdued. He stood by the door and calmly said, "May I come in?"

I hesitated a little, then opened the door more and told him, "Sure..."

"I heard you play the piano, it's so beautiful. I envy you! You can come up with these beautiful tunes any time you want."

"Do you want me to play something for you?"

I asked Sayed while smiling and trying to retrieve what I have memorized from modern Arabic music so that I could play it for him. I was hoping that our tastes in music could meet even in one thing, but I was surprised by him saying, "Could you play 'Overture' from 'The Marriage of Figaro'?"

I was amazed by Sayed's fine taste; he asked for a quite unique piece of music. It was a surprise for me to learn that he knew it in the first place.

"Mozart, Figaro, and Overture by name?! You have a taste for classical music, Sayed!"

"Excuse me, sir. But I used to listen to classical music for hours during my practice in college."

Mozart - Overture - The Marriage of Figaro

"Are you a college graduate, Sayed?"

"No, sir. I did not complete my education... I was studying to be an artist, a sculptor to be specific. I believe I would've become a great sculptor one day, but I lost my way ... I took the path of addiction, the road that only ends in an abyss ... and I'm going down towards it little by little."

"Believe me, Sayed, I know what you are talking about, and I feel sympathy for you. Many of my fellow musicians have been hit with the same plague. Some of them tried to rise and resist, while others surrendered until death devoured them."

"And I am waiting for death, sir. I pray for it every moment ... You can't imagine how painful it is for the successful to see his failure and the strong to witness his frailty, and I was successful and strong, but I lost my way and lost myself with it, and here I am taking a new way... towards the abyss."

"But let me ask you, what has thrown you down this dark path?"

"Bad friends, sir. As usual, and like all stories of addicts, the beginning is always with bad friends, and the end is with them as well. Have you heard of an addict who died in a house of worship or in a hospital? The end is always in a wasteland at the hands of a scoundrel giving him a farewell score. And I've had my share of bad friends, 'my buddies' as they used to call themselves. They tempted me with all sorts of fun that they did every night while I didn't know they existed! They tempted me with the money they scattered like dirt while my father licked the dirt to get a little money. I was nothing to these people, simply nothing! But it seems that the admiration I got from my professors as a talented artist and sculptor got these buddies to be 'interested' in me. They drowned me with fun and amusement, then they drowned me with women and liquor, then they drowned me with drugs, then they left me alone on the way to the abyss."

"What bastards they are! But you can still resist and come back to the right path, Sayed."

"No, sir. I have neither the stamina nor the desire to resist. I just want to leave this world as quickly as possible. Please, let's forget about me and listen to Mozart."

I started playing, and I continued playing for two hours, while Sayed kept sitting next to me, on the floor, leaning his head against the wall, with his eyes closed and his face relaxed and enjoying the music. After I finished, Sayed stood up and extended his hand to me. As soon as I extended my hand back to shake his, he bent down to kiss it.

I quickly pulled my hand away but he clung to it, telling me in a quavering voice, "I thank you... I thank you that you respected me and did not alienate or reprimand me. I promise I will try as hard not to repeat what I did on my first visit. I will not invade your privacy and I will not ask you for money... unless the whole world turns its back on me, and I can only find you for help."

I looked at Sayed trying to show sympathy rather than sadness, while he continued, "Sir, I am a worn-out rag with no dignity... but I still have remnants of morals that push me to respect people like you."

I did not answer, simply because I didn't know what to say. I slowly pulled my hand from Sayed's who came back to speak in his quavering voice,

"I have one last request. Please don't tell Madame Dina about my visit. Otherwise, my father will taste the bitterness of censuring or the humiliation of expulsion."

Sayed left, leaving a storm of thoughts in my head. This lost soul was on its way to the no return for sure. The basis of recovery from addiction is the sincere and strong desire of addicts to be cured. As for Sayed, he had a sincere and strong desire to die.

Days passed and the situation was the same, no acquaintances, no interviews, and no ladder for glory. My encounters with Dina became more infrequent, we hardly saw each other except in bed. She became so busy working in her studio and among her artworks which I knew nothing about. The artist's curiosity was pushing me relentlessly to see her works and learn about her sculptures, but she constantly and obstinately refused to show me or even tell me anything about them. In the evening, she was with her colleagues at their parties, for which she no longer offered to invite me, except on a few and sporadic occasions.

The only source of amusement in my life became the piano lessons, which I started to accept and even enjoy, and Sayed, who started visiting me frequently. And I have to admit it, we had nice times chatting when he was under the influence of Heroin, we talked about art and artists and many other subjects, until that day that turned everything upside down...

Lang Lang played 'La Campanella' from my phone. I quickly checked the caller's identity. It's a number I didn't know. I answered, "Hello."

"Hello, Hamdi, my dear friend."

It was Ihab. This bastard! I tried calling him several times and he never answered any of my calls.

"You jerk! For six months you didn't try to call me or answer my calls, even once. What's wrong with you?!"

"Excuse me, Hamdi. I was working hard to get my life together, and I finally did. I want to meet you as soon as possible."

"Set the time and place."

"Listen, your wife is having an art exhibition later this week. I'll be there, and I'll see you there and we'll talk."

"But, Dina didn't tell me anything about this exhibition. She seems so busy these days, but she hasn't told me anything."

"She will tell you, and she will definitely invite you to attend. She's just stalling until the last moment so as not to expose herself in front of you."

"What are you talking about?! What do you mean by exposing herself?!"

"Don't worry my friend. I'll tell you when I see you."

Ihab ended the call, leaving me with more questions and no answers. Oh, that bastard! From the first day I met Dina in the garden of his house, he's been talking riddles. In all our encounters there was always something he was trying to hide, and all our discussions ended up with me loaded with more questions and concerns than before, this call we just had was not different. His slippery way of talking made me forget to ask him if he had heard anything from Hans... Hans, Ihab and Dina... How despicable all of them are! They hide more in their sleeves than they show in their hands, and keep their secrets well hidden even if that secrecy is destructive to those around them.

I told Dina nothing; nothing about Ihab's call and nothing about this exhibition he told me about. And as that weasel had predicted, she told me about her exhibition the next day, "Bring all your savings from your music lessons. There will be an auction for my work, and you must participate and bid."

I looked at her with a smile that I tried to load it with confidence, and said, "Of course I'll attend your exhibition. I'll even bid as the rich do, and I'll get one of your fine works, at least."

Dina chuckled and said, "Oh, you poor thing! All the piano lessons in the world won't enable you to buy one of my works!"

'Your arrogance is killing me, Dina. I've never seen an ego that is so inflated as yours. I bet no one can make a statue of you, Dina. Simply because there is not enough stone on earth to sculpt your vanity.' That was what I said, to myself of course.

The day before the exhibition was a busy one. Dina brought several workers to carry her stone carvings to the exhibition area. I kept watching the workers carry the huge sculptures and groaning under the weight of them. I used to see the workers transporting rocks and stones to the workshop, and Dina would take them from time to time to buy the raw materials she used in the workshop. But this time it was different, Dina carefully covered the sculptures, and I couldn't see —or even discern— what they looked like.

In the evening Sayed came knocking, but it was not a friendly visit, at least in the beginning. He was in a very agitated state; he didn't find any money for his drugs, so he had to come to me. He was crying like a child and his drool was pouring from his mouth and falling onto his chest. I gave him the money he needed, so he rushed away on staggering feet, only to come back two hours later. He came back farther from agitation and closer to the abyss.

"I suppose, Sayed, you would kill whoever pushed you down the path of addiction if you saw him again."

Sayed looked at me with cloudy eyes, then smiled and mumbled, "His name is Hani, I still see him from time to time, and sometimes he even shows kindness and gives me dope in exchange for me washing his car."

"You see him, Sayed?! And serve him too?!!"

"I'm ready to sacrifice anything to reach the abyss, and here I am approaching it one dose at a time, and if this sinful wicked bastard will help me reach my demise quicker, then I should thank him."

I couldn't find an answer to Sayed's argument so I kept my mouth shut. His talk was full of despair but it was right. If this was the path he was determined to take in all cases, then why delaying the inevitable?

Sayed remained silent for a while, then closed his eyes and said, "He is one of Madame Dina's friends."

His words fell on my head like a heavy hammer.

"What do you mean?!"

Sayed opened his eyes, looked at the ceiling, closed them back and started telling me his miserable story, "I was in the first year of college, and Madame Dina and Hani were in their senior year. Although we were supposed to be colleagues in the same college, Madame Dina kept avoiding me like a plague, and she had every right to do so; she wanted to study sculpture abroad but failed. In the end, she was accepted into an institute of fine arts in Paris, only to be expelled four months later... and in the world of fine art, being expelled from such a place is like being expelled from heaven... no reputable place would accept you after that, so she had come back here to finish her study, and there I was, the son of Radi the housekeeper, entering the same college and becoming her peer. I was a disgrace to her, so she avoided talking to me and denied that she even knew me, and I was so happy with her attitude. Your wife, and I am sorry to say it, is the one person everybody wishes to keep away from. However, it seemed that my skills and talent, which were clear from the first days of study, caught the attention of her friends, including Hani, and he was the one who pushed me to this path and the first to guide me to the abyss."

I laid in my bed alone, thinking about what Sayed had said tonight. Dina was at the exhibition and would have to spend the night there to prepare for the opening in the morning. This gave me the time and space I needed to absorb the disturbing and devastating story of this poor Sayed and deal with the hundred questions that bombarded my brain. Why did this Hani treat Sayed as his best friend, giving him his attention and offering him his friendship, only to dump him later? And why did life treat Sayed as a rising star, indulging him with talent and offering him a bright career, only to turn its face on him later? And if Hani had his own reasons for this change of heart, being probably a moody and restless person like most of those in his social class, what was the excuse for fate to turn its back on Sayed leaving him to sniff his way to death? And the most important question was ... Why did Dina's name keep surfacing whenever there was someone I know suffering?!

The Deceived

"I remembered my meeting with Hans. I remembered his obvious admiration for my skill. I remembered how close I was to my dream. I realized how stupid and naïve I was. I thought I was an opportunity hunter, only to find myself the prey."

In the morning I went to the gallery where Dina was exhibiting her work. Although I was there early, I found a good number of attendees who arrived before me, and more visitors kept coming by the minute. I didn't know that there were many people interested in the art of sculpture. I saw Dina from a distance, she was talking passionately to some of the attendees and pointing to one of her exhibited pieces just as artists and painters do when they show their work. I thought that I, as a musician, was much luckier than these poor artists; I didn't need an explanation or demonstration for my work, and I didn't need to entertain my attendees or even care about them. All I needed to do was to tackle my black and white keys so that the tones emanate from them, then I let the audience gasp behind my tunes and my music without explanation or persuasion.

I stopped comparing artists to musicians and started touring the exhibition. I was so curious to see Dina's work that she has been hiding from me since we got married. So I took this opportunity to take a walk in the exhibition area, looking at every piece and examining each work she made. I was not an expert in fine arts, and I didn't know much about the art of sculpture in precise, especially the contemporary sculptural school. All my experience was derived from previous readings, a few galleries and some colleagues in the field, plus the several parties I attended with Dina where I saw her colleagues displaying their work or pictures of it.

Again, I was not an expert, and I didn't know much about this art. That was what I kept telling myself to lull my mind, which was screaming in my ears at the top of its voice. I was trying to calm it down and deny what it was screaming with, but my stubborn brain was holding to its opinion and proclaiming it with all its might... This was not art! It was not art! nor Sculpture! It was nothing! absolutely nothing! Those were freaks! Those were disfigured forms devoid of any kind of talent and lacking any form of creativity! Could Dina be that incompetent? Could she be that bad as a sculptor, and that ignorant as an artist? What about the inspiration nonsense she used to fill my ears with? What about the hours and hours she spent in her workshop? And what about this exhibition? This was a waste of time, effort and stone! Either I was so ignorant and tasteless, or it was really what I thought. That was not an art exhibition... that was a disaster!

A hand patting my shoulder woke me from that nightmare I was drowning into, and which was getting more ominous and more terrifying the more I thought of it. Thank God. It was Ihab.

"Hamdi my dear friend!"

I decided to seize this opportunity of finally meeting this slippery bastard, so I pushed my mind to focus on my music, on Hans, and on the road to glory... and let the whole lousy exhibition and all Dina's disfigured idols burn in hell.

I replied to Ihab saying, "Here you are finally! I thought I was the worst friend ever, but you beat me to this title!"

"Sorry, my friend. I really couldn't talk to you earlier. Come on, let's get out of here."

"But what about this exhibition?!"

"Don't worry. This will be here when you get back, and your wife will be busy with her guests the whole day."

Despite all my efforts to keep my focus on my own career, my mind insisted on getting back to this disaster called exhibition. So I said to Ihab, "Ihab, did you notice anything odd about this exhibition?!"

"My dear, this is not an exhibition... This is a farce! Come and I will tell you everything."

Ihab and I went outside. He walked calmly and silently while I was dying of curiosity to know what this mysterious bastard was hiding, and what happened with Hans who disappeared as well. We headed to a nearby café. We ordered two cups of coffee. I talked and asked, trying to understand what was going on around me, and Ihab responded with a few short words. Finally, after about a quarter of an hour of useless talk, Ihab took a big sip of his coffee and left it in his mouth for a little while, then swallowed it all at once and started talking... the talk that would turn my life upside down.

"Listen, Hamdi. you are the only friend whose friendship I truly cherish, and God knows that you are the only one whom I respect and admire among my friends..."

"Ihab—"

"Please do not interrupt me. What I am doing now is heavy on myself and stressful to my heart, but it has to be done, so let me finish my words. During the past six months I have been trying to convince my father to let me continue learning music abroad. The man was determined to make me leave the music business and become a true businessman like my brothers, but I refused. I began writing to music institutes abroad so that I might find a place for myself in one of them. Finally, I was accepted into the 'Jacobs School of Music' in Indiana. I am traveling at the end of the month."

I didn't utter a word. I felt this was all an introduction to what was much more critical and much more painful. I was right...

"I am not traveling to study music because I love it, but to get away from this dirty and dishonest world in which I live. I have always pictured my father and my older brothers as Gods ... strong, brave, smart, but I was surprised when I became more involved in their business and saw the way they ran it ... They are rats! Ugly and dirty rats. They bully the weak and gasp in fear of the strong. Their consciences abhor lawful gains and subsist on dirty opportunities. I know and confess that I have many, many bad qualities, but such extreme hypocrisy and total dishonesty are not among them, so I am traveling to get away from this rotten atmosphere."

My stomach twisted and my heart started pounding. For sure, Ihab did not come today to tell me about his issues with his family. This was all an introduction for the bad news he was bringing to me. Ihab kept talking, "Hamdi, I am leaving and not caring about anything or anyone. I convinced my father to put an amount of money in my account that would suffice me for all the years of schooling. Now I don't care if he triples his fortune or he declares bankruptcy. Rather, I hope that everything he and my brothers own would disappear. Because falsehood must remain false no matter what. The only person I feel sorry for is you! You, Hamdi. God gave you the talent and the stamina to be a truly world-class artist and a genius musician, then he stripped you of the means to capture your dream, and made you beg for your way to glory even though you are more deserving of it than all of us. Even when I tried to help you, fate pushed this damned Dina in your way to take you down in her own dark and ugly maze, and you fell down, Hamdi! You fell into the traps of this cursed chameleon. You surrendered to her with your naivety and inexperience. You thought she would be your way to flourish ... but in fact, it is your way to perish..."

"Ihab, please! Dina is my wife now, and what you say to me now about her makes me..."

"Dina called Hans, Hamdi. She called him after she met you and after she felt that you would be falling in her trap, she called to threaten him if he tried to contact you or include you in his school, she threatened him to keep away from you. Otherwise, she would pressure her family to stop funding his school. The man called me out of courtesy and told me this while he was fuming, not only because he admires you and wants you in his school, but also because he's not used to being put in such a strange and awkward situation, or to being dictated and given orders in such a crude and shameless way."

Ihab's words were falling on my head like hammers falling on molten steel. My mind stopped thinking and went wailing and crying, I felt the world revolving around me and my body was getting cold, beads of sweat were running down my forehead, I said to Ihab with a heavy tongue, "But... why all this?!"

"Haven't you realized yet, Hamdi?! Dina is not the typical narcissist or the average selfish person that you hear about everyday. Dina makes Narcissus disgusted by her narcissism and makes King Leopold terrified of her selfishness and desire to destroy others to please herself."

Ihab turned his seat and leaned towards me. He looked me straight in the eyes and continued, "Dina has convinced you that she will be your gateway to glory, when in fact she was taking you as her gateway to her own glory! Dina was not able to break into the world of art from any of its doors. She was not accepted by any of the real artists; painters, sculptors, photographers, you name it! All avoided her for her talentless work and her tactless behavior. She tried to relate herself to sculptors, but they quickly pushed her away after they saw her works, her freaky works that you see in this farce that she calls an exhibition."

I didn't know what to say and I didn't want to say anything, I just wanted him to continue talking, and he did.

"So this wily old fox decided to look for a real artist, a talented one, an artist that people would admire and want to befriend, an artist they would welcome into their community, and they would welcome her back because she was related to him, an artist that would be accepted by the sculptors but is not in the same field so as not to compete with her for the spotlights. Let him be a musician, for example!"

"You mean I was..."

"You were that person, my dear. You were that person. It was my fault that I invited her to the party you and Hans attended, but my biggest mistake was that I had acceded to her urgent requests to invite so many artists in her field, which she has been desperately trying to get close to, while they've been avoiding her all the time. After you played your lovely music in front of Hans, many of them wanted to know you and have you in their social circle, and to invite you to come to their parties and gatherings. I tried to keep you away from that atmosphere, so I kept myself away from you that night, but this damned woman picked up the tip of the string and took advantage of how the social circle that she's been dying to enter is now opening to you."

"You... You should've told me..."

"I couldn't, Hamdi. I couldn't. The first thing she did was get me out of the picture; she sent me a clear message not to talk with you and to keep away, and I had to obey because of her father's influence on my family's business. Then, she appointed herself as your 'social agent'! She called everyone she was hopelessly chasing, and who listened to you playing and admired your talent, she invited them to many parties in your name and re-introduced herself as your today's fiancé and your future wife. She used to tell you that she was taking you to 'her' parties, when in fact it was you taking her to 'your' parties! People started accepting her existence only because of you and your true and genuine talent. You were her gateway into the world of art and artists, the world that she ran after and did not belong to."

I spoke... I replied to Ihab, not because I had anything to say, but just to talk and to make sure I was still awake and sane.

I spoke but didn't know what to say because of the many punches and slams that hit my already melted head.

"But... Dina doesn't need all this!"

"No, my dear. She is in dire need of all this. You have your ambitions and desires that Dina has succeeded in manipulating, taking advantage of your ignorance of the world of applied art; a world that knows very well her limited capabilities and her lack of talent. You see, Dina is not only lacking talent and tactfulness, she also lacks morals and integrity. In her college years, she took advantage of the weakness and need of others and made them work on her graduation projects, bypassing many real artists. Then in the start of her career she bribed and manipulated votes to reap many awards that she did not even deserve to touch, infringing on the rights of many talented sculptors. But after a while, she discovered that her reputation in the art community was totally smeared. She had no way to survive in this milieu except to perform a complete public relation makeover that would change her image and make her closer to the hearts of this community members, and you were the makeup artist who did this amazing makeover."

"But... with her money... she could've..."

"In this milieu, Hamdi, money buys you prizes but does not buy praise. It buys devious certification but not sincere appreciation. The problem with Dina is that she's done so many wrongs at the beginning that caused the art community to shut her out, she needed access back and a seat on the table. She knew that she could 'negotiate' her way back to this community once she was in, but she needed access first, something to make her more 'palatable' and acceptable to the group, and you were this access."

"... and Hans?"

"Hans was the greatest challenge she faced, for if the man had accepted you in his school, you would have traveled immediately, and then you would've not considered her offer of marriage, and hence you would've not done your part in her plan. So, she threatened Hans to keep away from you, and then hastened the marriage so that Hans would know that she has become your wife and that your subject was closed. She is good, Hamdi. She is good. The one thing your wife does better than setting diabolical plans is executing them with marvellous precision."

My reckless greed tried to defend Dina one more time, and one last time.

"But, Ihab... the exhibition, the invitees, the attendance... the auction! Dina must have at least a little talent to do all that."

Ihab sadly smiled, as he threw the last bomb on the wreckage of my dreams.

"My dear, all that you see today is a scam... a lie ... a meticulously drawn hoax! Dina's works lying there in the exhibition are devoid of any artistic flair, and her gigantic sculptures are idols that symbolize nothing. The old idols of 'Quraysh' made of date were deeper in art and more refined in taste than the works of this shallow, talentless woman."

"... and the audience?"

"They are all like me. Either from her relatives, or employees of her father's companies, or those who have business interests with him. Each came today to fulfill a specific task assigned to him. My task today is to bid on a specific piece; Number eight. I'll start bidding on it, and some bidders will try to outbid me, until the price reaches fifty-five thousand, this is the hammer price, then the bidders will withdraw, and I will win this 'precious' piece of bloody art, to the applause and admiration of the audience."

I felt a glimpse of happiness despite all these brutal blows pouring on my head. I was happy because I was, finally, right in one thing; Dina's work had nothing to do with art and carried nothing related to talent. Ihab continued talking, "But this is not the highest price you'll see today. Pieces 9 to 12 each will sell each for one million pounds! Do you know why? Because this auction is actually a money laundry! Laundering part of the money of Dina's father's company among other companies; they buy the work of this moron as masterpieces and then resell it! And their dirty money enters the gallery only to come out clean."

"This is wrong... No... This is a crime! There must be something to do..."

"Hamdi, please don't lose your temper and do something that you'd regret for the rest of your life. Be patient and play along. See where all of this will lead you. For me, all of this no longer concerns me now, I am traveling, leaving behind this farce forever, but if you honor my father and do not want him to get in harm, please do not involve me in this matter and do not involve my name in anything I have told you."

That was too much for me to handle. My heart pounded so vigorously and my brain was numb. But I had to get back to my own issues. I had to understand from Ihab about my fate with this wretch.

"You mean that Dina will use me to fix her miserable image in front of her colleagues, and then get rid of me after my mission is over?"

"Oh, my friend! I wish... I wish she would do that. If she had intended to get rid of you after she's done with you then I would not have spoken to you in the first place. I would've let her divorce you after a month or two, and then the ban will be lifted and Hans can invite you to his school, and all you would have lost is six months of your life."

"Then what do you think she will do?"

"It seems that this serpent has feelings for you! And she decided to keep you by her side forever. I learned from my family's lawyer that she is taking some measures to keep you on her side forever. I myself don't know what she intends to do, all I know is that she has no intention to let you go."

"Do you mean I will remain under her thumb all my life?"

"And under her eyes as well! Let me tell you one last thing that is important for you to know, Dina uses the security staff at her father's company to keep an eye on people she wants to monitor. When we were young, she would often come to the club to tell me about all my moves and whereabouts the day before, and I was fascinated by her divine ability to know what the 'rest of humanity' was doing, until I grew up and learned that this manipulating wicked is using the poor security personnel in her father's company to watch whomever she wanted to watch..."

Ihab didn't finish his sentence. At this point, my nerves couldn't stand it, I remembered my meeting with Hans. I remembered his obvious admiration for my skill. I remembered how close I was to my dream. I realized how stupid and naïve I was. I thought I was an opportunity hunter, only to find myself the prey.

I blew out of my place like a raging bull and grabbed Ihab by his lapel while screaming, "How did you leave me, you damned bastard? How did you let me swallow her bait like a goof? Why didn't you warn me? you despicable."

Ihab grabbed my hand and quietly removed his clothes from my fingers as he said, "I warned you, Hamdi. Indeed, I warned you. Remember the words that I said to you that day ... Say that you are traveling, say that you are ill, even say that you are queer if you have to! But don't let her spin her web around you ... remember those words? I did warn you, my friend, but you did not listen to my warnings, and I was ready to warn you more, but the look of greed and clinginess which I saw in your eyes that night stopped me from elaborating further, it was obvious that you would never listen to me. Dina threw her nets around you and you gladly and willingly fell in it. All that I was hoping for was for this cunning to use you for a while and then let you go, but it seems that she decided to leave you writhing next to her until she takes your last breath."

Ihab got up from his seat and headed back to the exhibition, but I couldn't get up. Was it my brain so paralyzed it couldn't order my feet to carry me? Or was it my nerves that were so burned so they couldn't carry the order to stand up? Or was it me realizing that there was no sense of standing up now after all what I learned about my gullibility and foolishness? I stayed in my seat, in the café... alone. I cursed my naivety and my inexperience. I cursed my greed and rapacity. I cursed Hans and his cowardice. I cursed Ihab and his reluctance to help me... and I cursed her... cursed her... cursed her... the despicable... the sordid... brimful of deception and evil... empty of talent or creativity. She annihilated my future to turn me into a puppet; a puppet that she won't let go even after she was done playing with it. Oh, you Dina... May you burn in eternal flames. May you die as a soul and as a memory, and only your stinky carcass remains... but I... I will live... I will evolve... I will be introducing my music in Paris and Vienna, and you will be introducing your body as food for worms and earth. I will reach my glory destined to me... and you will not live to see it... you will not live... I will make sure you will not live.

I suddenly remembered my brother, Hassan... He also went through many betrayals and suffered many disappointments, but he would let his rage and disappointment eat his body and soul, he would revolt, lather and foam, and then end up in ruins. I remembered Hassan and his fate and promised myself never to surrender to my wrath and outrage. I then remembered my sister, Hanan ... She was the one who planned it all, in patience and in poise, until she got what she wanted. I remembered Hanan and her success and promised myself never to let my feelings overpower my wisdom. I might have been naive, but I was not stupid, my only mistake was that I had faith in Dina, believed her nonsense and trusted her promises, but now the game was all clear to me, and I was determined to win it, and she would be the one regretting it, if she lived long enough to regret anything.

The fervor of retaliation and lust for revenge overcame my sense of helplessness and failure, so I stood up and started walking back towards the gallery. There was one step I had to take; I had to make sure that Ihab's claims were true, so I decided to attend the auction and see how it goes. I arrived at the exhibition by the time the auction was starting, I sat in the back rows watching the auction progress ... the sixth piece, the seventh, the eighth. Bidding has started on the eighth item ... ten thousand from Ihab, fifteen thousand from another bidder, twenty from the third bidder, twenty-five, thirty. Ihab returned to the bidding race, thirty-five, another bidder raised him with forty-five. Ihab went up to fifty-five... a la uno... a la due... a la tre! Ihab Azzam... fifty-five thousand... item number eight ... the original alabaster statue called 'The Deceived'!

Oh, Ihab... You bastard! Couldn't you find a totem to bid on except this ugly one called 'The Deceived'?! Did you have to bid on me?! Ihab's words were true, everything he told me was either true by evidence or proper by common sense. It was my call then, and I called for revenge; revenge that must be planned wisely and stealthily, and served cold and slowly. There was no time to break down and cry, and there was no time for anger and rage either. I needed to think. I needed to plan. And I, desperately, needed some fresh air, an air that hadn't been defiled by Dina's devilish breaths.

Hani

"The only difference between Hani and Sayed was that the latter could not buy enough Heroin to meet the raging needs burning his blood, while Hani did not have enough blood to absorb all the Heroin he could buy, but the two were speeding towards the abyss."

I walked out of the fair and went back to the café. I needed some peace of mind to gather my thoughts and plan my next move...

"Hamdi..."

The last thing I needed at that moment was someone to interrupt my thoughts, but there was no way not to respond. I turned to see who was calling me, I remembered that face, he was one of the regular attendees of Dina's parties, but there was no chance for us to get acquainted. "What does this idiot want from me?" I said to myself, all I wanted at this moment was to be left alone with my thoughts. But this nosy person insisted on intruding.

I looked back. It was a man in his late twenties, although his skinny body and his whisker shredded jeans gave him the look of a teenager rather than an adult.

I knew that I have seen that face before, but I couldn't remember when and where. He saved me the trouble of trying to squeeze my already scrambled mind to remember him.

"Hamdi. I don't think you remember me. We quickly met at a gathering of mutual friends."

"I remember you, but we didn't talk, so I'm sorry I don't remember the name."

"It's okay, my name is Hani."

Hani... the name pierced my ear to awaken the remaining of my already-burning brain cells, could this wicked be Hani, Sayed's demon and his guide to the abyss?

"Hello, Hani. You seem to be a close friend of Dina; You are the only one from the parties I attended that I could see at the exhibition today."

"Indeed. I am Dina's closest friend. I hope that the word 'closest friend' does not encroach upon or transgress you."

"Never mind, Hani. Are you Dina's college classmate?"

"Yes. I am her classmate. Same class, same year of graduation."

The new fire was still devouring what was left of my mind and what was left of my nerves. For sure this was Sayed's Hani... Hani who overpowered poor Sayed and pushed him into the abyss. Another bloody name to be added to the list of damned.

But I kept my anger under control for the thousandth time today. I said to myself 'Control yourself. Patience and planning, Hamdi, patience and planning. This damned Dina planned to set you up, so you also plan to set her up, and pouring out your anger on Hani would never serve your plan or help you achieve anything, so use this opportunity to learn more about Dina and her wrongdoings from her close and intimate friend.'

"Hani. I'm going for coffee at a nearby café, would you join me?"

"On the contrary. Let's do anything but stay in this gallery... I mean... I love fine art, but I hate exhibitions."

We walked together and chatted until we reached the café. We ordered coffee and started talking. I tried to forget the conversation that took place between me and Ihab for the sake of getting this Hani to open up to me and show me the skeletons in his and Dina's closets.

So I put all my focus on observing Hani and listening to his talk, and this idiot loved to talk! It was evident from the first moment that he was so simple, so spontaneous, and so junkie! His sunken eyes were fiery red, his heavy tongue was fighting to get words out in the right order, his emaciated body and his slow movements, all indicated that it was Heroin, not wisdom that resided in the blood of this Hani.

The only difference between him and Sayed was that the latter could not buy enough Heroin to meet the raging needs burning his blood, while Hani did not have enough blood to absorb all the Heroin he could buy, but the two were speeding towards the abyss.

Our chat over coffee ended with us becoming friends, or so that damned Hani imagined.

"Hamdi, I feel that this is the beginning of a solid and strong friendship, and I am so happy to become a friend to a talented artist like you. All I wish is for our friendship to stay away from Dina. I don't want her to be jealous of her husband or of her colleague."

I smiled as I looked at Hani. I remembered Ihab's words, "I will tell you things but don't tell Dina," I remembered Sayed's words, "I will come to visit you but don't tell Dina," and here was Hani joining the list of those who were afraid of her, "Let's all be friends and buddies. But don't tell Dina." Everyone seemed to be afraid of Dina, but do they hate her the same way I did?

I kept smiling as I said to Hani, "Rest assured, my friend, I am the last one to inform his wife about his friendships."

Hani hurried back to the exhibition, while I chose to return to the villa. I wouldn't be able to look at Dina in the face after all that I learned today. I needed to be alone for a while. I was walking aimlessly as my mind was busy checking today's aftermath, so all it could do was to let my feet lead me wherever they wanted.

* * *

Finally, I got to the villa and headed to the third floor, or my so-called hermitage. I needed to vent my burning anger, so I started playing Prokofiev's Suggestion Diabolique. I played it once, twice, and three times, but Prokofiev did not manage to empty the fire inside me. I played Bartók's Allegro barbaro. By the time I finished playing it, my nerves were completely burnt! I no longer had any energy to fuel my anger. My mind has become clearer and calmer. Now I can think, my revenge from her must be very hideous, but it mustn't affect me. I will not hurt myself while hurting her. I will crush her and get myself out unharmed.

First, I needed to make sure that she was not putting me under her silly surveillance. I planned to share with her my daily schedule until she would become comfortable knowing my whereabouts. She should get used to my absence and feel comfortable leaving me alone.

Allegro Barbaro (Sz.49)
Béla Bartók

Suggestion Diabolique
Prokofiev

I also planned to accept new students for piano lessons, which would allow me to get away from her and her eyes. And will give me time and space to be away from her control.

It was important to get to know this bastard Hani, he seemed to know a lot about her, and he must have some of her dirty secrets that I could use against her.

I decided at thats moment to rest and get some sleep. My whole body was groaning from the shocks of this difficult day, and my mind was begging me to rest. Sometimes when one's life is falling apart, the best thing to do is to sleep it off. I entered my room, lay on the bed, and fell into a deep sleep despite all the gloomy thoughts bombarding my brain.

I woke up to the sound of knocking on the door. I don't know what time it was, but it was night. I sluggishly dragged my feet to open the door. It was Sayed.

"Very sorry. Have I woken you up?"

With this calm attitude and these good manners, I could definitely tell that Sayed was under the influence of Heroin.

"No. No worries. Come in."

I spent two hours chatting with Sayed. I still wanted to learn about him and his story. I tried to further understand the nature of his relationship with Hani, and why would this Hani, the spoiled rat, care about befriending this poor Sayed. I felt a strange urge to learn about this odd couple, despite all the upheavals I went through today, and despite my burning nerves and my broken dreams.

Even with all the deep sleep that had just swallowed me up earlier, as soon as Sayed left I found myself falling asleep again. I only woke up at nine in the morning, it was Mr. Lang Lang and 'La Campanella' that woke me up.

"Hello. Mr. Hamdi?"

It was a beautiful voice of a woman. A voice carrying a youthful tone and at the same time the poise and confidence of an experienced woman. I answered curiously, "Yes, Madam."

"I am Ingie. My daughter, Malak, loves piano, and she wants to continue learning piano at the hands of a Grandmaster like you."

"Madam, please. This is an honor I do not claim to reach, the title of Grandmaster is a dream for those like me, and if I were a Grandmaster, I would never have thought of giving piano lessons."

Her laughter rose over the phone. Oh men, we let our guard down in front of the alluring laughter of any female, even if it was over the phone.

We agreed that I would come to her house and meet Malak in the afternoon. I didn't ask her about the age of Malak, not even if she had a piano or not! Ingie's feminine and tempting voice and her pampered laughter were enough to convince me to go and meet her. There was no comparison between her warm voice that was brimful of softness and seduction, and Dina's damned voice that was packed with firm orders and false confidence.

But... Where was that Dina?! I started searching for her in the villa but couldn't find her. This mean and wicked witch! She spent the night away and didn't even bother to tell me. But this was not the time for anger, even if it was justified anger. Patience and planning were what I needed, patience and planning. I grabbed my phone and texted her, "My love. Where are you?

I woke up and couldn't find you home. I am worried. Please call."

I threw the phone aside. I didn't care if she replied or not, I didn't even care if she spent her night in hell!

I went to make myself some coffee, but a message had arrived on my phone, "Sorry. I had to stay with my parents until all the work related to the exhibition is over, I'll be home in the evening." Finally, a piece of good news! I would rest from seeing her until tomorrow, I needed that time to get myself together.

I drank my coffee to the melodies of the 'Lacrimosa'. 'Requiem' was the one piece of music that I loved as much as I loved playing the piano. It was the wonderful masterpiece of Mozart; Wolfgang Amadeus Mozart, the greatest composer of all times in my opinion. And as Mozart was a legendary composer, his 'Requiem' was a legendary piece of music with a legendary story; a nobleman asked him to attribute it to himself in lamenting his wife, and Mozart was at the time suffering from poverty and need, so he was forced to take the offer. Mozart put all his genius and talent in the 'Requiem', as he had a strong and overwhelming feeling then that this would be his last piece of music to compose. He believed he had been cursed to write a requiem as a swansong for himself, because he was sure he was about to die, so he considered it as his own requiem, honoring his own death.

Indeed, he died before he could complete it! And the 'Requiem' came into existence as the best and most wonderful incarnation of death and resurrection. The talents of great musicians were resurrected every time their music was played, while those of mediocre ones would die once their bodies were buried. For me, my talent and passion seemed to be buried even before my body, with no requiem to eternise my music or a mass to memorise my talent.

Mozart - Lacrimosa

Ingie

"You do not need all this vulgarity, woman! Keep your decency, your message has been delivered."

At six I was standing in front of Madame Ingie's house, a villa smaller than Dina's, albeit superior in beauty and taste, surrounded by a wonderful garden dotted with jasmine trees. I didn't know if the secret was in the design of the villa or if it was the wonderful garden, but it was certainly a place that inspired comfort and intimacy.

I knocked on the door and a lady opened for me. She was Madame Ingie, or so I wished. A beautiful woman in the truest sense of the word; fate gave her a beautiful face, and the hands of plastic surgeons contributed to its retouching and preservation. The same goes for her body which was a gorgeous, invoking thoughts of Aphrodite, and the hands of plastic surgeons once again helped reveal the charms of this beautiful body, pushing it away from the angelical and into the diabolical sect. From her side, she did not skimp on this demonic body with clothes that revealed more than they concealed, turning her into a goddess of temptation and femininity

I couldn't help but remember Dina. This wicked woman strived hard so that your eyes could see her beauty, but with Ingie every piece of her was screaming with charm.

"Mr. Hamdi?"

"Yes. Madame Ingie?"

"Yes. Come in, please."

It was her, and her I was going to get. This woman would be my prey, I would win her to satisfy the desire that caught up with me the moment I saw her. I would win to humiliate Dina and destroy her huge ego. I will betray Dina with this perfect woman, and let the flames of jealousy and heartbreak eat your black heart, Dina.

I entered the hall only to find a lovely young lady standing there and waiting for me, she must be Malak; a girl of sixteen years of age, who got the beautiful and innocent looks of her mothers without the diabolical touches of plastic surgeons, she looked like an elegant and delicate butterfly. Her smile revealed her tenderness and kindness which made her closer to angels than to humans. She was standing next to a grand piano that added to her elegance and grace.

As soon as I saw her, my dirty thoughts about seducing her mother retreated and disappeared, only to be replaced by feelings of disgust at myself and my filthy mind. How could I think like that to the mother of such innocence and purity? As if Malak had immediately become my sound moral and my living conscience.

I was surprised by Malak's advanced information about music. I learned from her that she had finished studying solfège a long time ago and that she had a great deal of mastery at playing the piano. But Madame Ingie insisted on explaining Malak's skill in playing the piano by herself.

"Malak has studied music and playing piano in America since she was five years old, as we were living with her father there, and after the separation we came back here, and I want her to continue her piano lessons."

My filthy thoughts resurfaced to play with my mind and to tickle my lust, Ingie wasted no time before telling me that she was separated from her husband. What a playful woman!

Malak started playing piano, and chose Beethoven's masterpiece 'Für Elise' to begin with, a piece of the highest delicacy and charm, and the pinnacle of cunning! Its beginning was simple; an easy note that repeated itself, however it would expose any inexperienced or insensitive player as it needed a lot of training and talent to show its true richness and content. This simple note was followed by a very difficult part that only talented and experienced fingers could master, but Malak played it with all smoothness and fluency.

Für Elise - Beethoven

As soon as Malak finished playing, I looked at Ingie saying, "Malak is excellent! She is even above excellent; she is a conservatoire student level who can easily become a competitor student. She's really talented! It is clear that she trains regularly and persistently, and if she continues, she will be a great pianist one day, and it is an honor for me to be her piano teacher."

"She is my daughter. She is like me in her love for piano and her musical ear, not only in beauty!"

Ingie said it as if it was a joke, but the look in her eyes fixed on mine, and the way she was standing in front of me with her arms crossed in front of her chest, confirmed that it was more than a joke. It might be my hormones speaking, but a flirtatious woman has a smell that no man can miss, no matter how naïve he was, and the smell of Madame Ingie's crazy desire was all over the place.

We agreed to start Malak's piano lessons the next day, and for three lessons every week. On the next day I was at Madame Ingie's villa on time, but this time I didn't come empty-handed; I brought a modern piano music collection as a gift for Malak, and a large bouquet of flowers for her mother.

Ingie met me at the door with a big, welcoming smile, and with a big 'Wow' for my wonderful gift, as she described it. She also met me with a dress that was lecherous and obscene, to say the least!

"This Demon wastes no time and leaves no doubt! She wants me... Now!" I almost told her that in her face; her face that, together with her body and her movements, were sending me all kinds of flirty messages. You did not need all that vulgarity, woman! Keep your decency, your message has been delivered.

I started the lesson with Malak. I sat next to her in front of the piano while Madame Ingie sat in front of us reading a magazine.

"May I smoke?"

Ingie asked with a smile. I smiled back and said, "Madame Ingie, this is your home and I am your guest. So, please do whatever you like."

Ingie smiled and took out a long, colorful cigarette and lit it. I didn't know that 'Nat Sherman' cigarettes were available here. Ingie quietly puffed her cigarette as she looked at me, she seemed to be checking me out, her looks gave me goosebumps. It was the hunter's looks to the prey. Madam Ingie, please don't mix the roles! In our next sinful relationship, I would be the hunter. I've played the role of the prey before, and it was devoid of fun and lacking excitement.

The lesson ended, so I saluted Malak and asked Madame Ingie's permission to leave. Ingie grabbed my elbow as she led me to the door. She stood at the entrance and leaned her back against the wall. She looked at me and said, "I'm feeling so comfortable in your presence, Mr. Hamdi. Please allow me to talk to you from time to time away from piano lessons. I need your opinion on some of my personal matters. From your side, please consider me your friend from now on, and please feel free to talk to me about whatever you need to talk about."

At this moment, and based on the way she stood, talked and dressed, I was supposed to take advantage of her and take the first step towards that dirty affair that was about to start. But instead, I curbed my desire and asked permission to leave. Patience and planning, Hamdi, patience and planning. However, I was sure I couldn't hold myself back for long.

* * * *

In the evening, Dina gave me some happy news. She received an invitation to talk about her 'successful' exhibition and her latest work from a 'private' showroom in London, so she was going to be traveling for a week.

"Would you like to come with me, Hamdi? London is beautiful this time of the year."

"No, my love. You go and enjoy London, enjoy showing your wonderful art and your beautiful works, and I will wait for you here."

Your wonderful art, and your beautiful works. Go, you talentless wicked. May you not come back! I was one step away from Hans' School, one step away from realizing my dream, a dream that you killed in cold blood. You killed it while deluding me that you were making it come true... Go, you, damned woman.

* * * *

A couple of days have passed. It was Malak's piano lesson. I went to the villa but this time without gifts, I went up the stairs and knocked on the door, and the courtesan opened for me! Yes, The courtesan. There was no other description to use to describe Ingie. The nightgown that she was wearing gave her that title with full merit. The previous dress I saw earlier was sending signals and hints, while this nightgown explicitly screamed an invitation to debauchery.

"Hello, Mr. Hamdi. I am so sorry. Malak went with the driver to visit one of her friends, but she got stuck in traffic on the way back. I don't think she'll be more than half an hour late. Please come in. Let's sit and talk until..."

Ingie couldn't finish her sentence, I silenced her with a kiss I forced on her lips, a kiss in which I put all my anger, my frustration, and my lust.

Few but flaming seconds had passed. Slowly I opened my eyes to look at Ingie's beautiful face and check her reaction to my well-invited, ill-planned kiss. I found her eyes closed and her lips clenched as if they were expecting more, I came back to kiss her again and empty in them all the madness I had inside me.

Ingie put her hands on my chest and gently pushed me away. She looked me in the eyes then grabbed my hand and opened the door of the villa. I thought at first that she intended to kick me out, but she was actually leading me to an annex that was almost separate from the villa.

She pulled me inside and closed the door. The annex had only one room... a bedroom.

I spent the happiest and dirtiest half hour of my life. I felt proud of my dishonesty and betrayal of that devil called Dina, and I felt proud of my filth and my triumph in bridling this wild mare called Ingie.

Time passed smutty and speedily, I got dressed in a hurry and rushed to the villa before Malak's arrival. Ingie followed me but dressed in a more modest and dignified garment, the slutty nightgown had done its job, and it was time for it to rest till our next 'lesson', though I didn't think Ingie would need it anymore to tempt me.

I quickly finished my piano lesson, saluted Malak and headed for the door. Ingie came to show me out, and to kiss me! She placed a quick kiss on my lips, whispering, "See you in two days... half an hour before class!"

I left her home feeling that I was Julius Caesar returning victoriously to Rome, with the sweet taste of glory and pride. Dina turned me into a soldier who obeyed her orders and fulfilled her desires without discussion, so there was no taste for victory or flavor for triumph with her, but with Ingie... I was the king.

I was the one in charge, in command. And I was the one celebrating all the victory and collecting all the spoils.

I went back to the villa. I slept like a little baby.

* * * *

Two days passed without anything new, music, coffee, piano lessons, music, coffee. Some calls from acquaintances I gained from Dina's parties, and a call from Hani inviting me to visit him the coming week. I tried to call Ihab several times but all my attempts were unsuccessful.

It was time for Malak's piano lesson, and the half-hour before class. The playful Aphrodite Ingie, and her slutty nightgown.

Ingie opened the door, she smiled viciously and said, "Malak is not home, again. Sorry!"

I stepped inside and caught Ingie in my arms, but she quickly winced and stepped back, pushing my hands while saying, "Not here... In the annex."

In the annex, we exchanged passion and love, but as soon as half an hour had passed, I found myself rising and hastening to get dressed so as not to be late for Malak's lesson. Ingie wanted to preserve the purity of Malak's house, so she was keeping all her sins in the annex. I in turn wanted to preserve the sanctity of Malak's lessons, so I wouldn't allow anything to make me late, even if it were the arms of Ingie. Oh, Malak. This girl lifted me up to virtue, while her mother pushed me down to vice.

I stood in front of the mirror to get dressed, while Ingie was lying in bed looking at me and smiling. She said, "What would happen if your wife found out about us?"

"She would kill us. She would kill you and then she would kill me. No, actually she would rape you, then she would rape me, and then she would kill us both."

Ingie released her feminine and seductive laughter and said, "Is that how jealous she gets?"

"It's not jealousy, dear... It's possessiveness!"

She replied as if she had not heard me, "I respect the woman who fights for her husband's fidelity, and I adore the man whose wife goes for this fight."

"Then adore me as you wish, my dear."

"You go to the villa, and I will catch up with you shortly."

It was obvious that she wanted to hide our affair from Malak, and I had the same feeling myself. I was afraid about Malak's feelings more than I was afraid from Dina if she found out about Ingie and I. I fixed my clothes, and hurried out of the annex and back to the villa.

Malak

"What had she seen and heard in this house that would grant her all this sad and woeful wisdom?"

I walked out of the annex door to the villa. I knocked on the door and Malak opened it for me. Without greetings or even smiling she said, "Mama's not here. Let's start the lesson until she comes."

Malak was talking to me with the utmost seriousness and strictness that did not suit her age. I smiled hesitantly and followed her to the piano. I kept asking myself, did this gentle butterfly know anything about my relationship with her mother?

"Let's start today with..."

I didn't finish my sentence, as Malak interrupted me sharply, "I want to play 'Confessions'."

"Lionel Yu! You have great taste, Malak, but it is a difficult piece and needs..."

Malak interrupted me for the second time, not with words she said but with notes she played. She began playing Lionel Yu's lovely piece 'Confessions'.

Her playing was amazing, it made me dive into the music and swim between the notes, remembering my true passion... the piano. Suddenly, Malak stopped playing. She looked at me sadly, then suddenly tears started to shine in her eyes.

I asked her earnestly, "What's wrong, Malak? What's bothering you?"

"I know... I know what's going on between you and my mother!"

My tongue was caught by surprise and my brain was paralyzed by the jolt, so I did not reply. But Malak insisted on continuing this extremely uncomfortable and shocking discussion.

Confessions - Lionel Yu

"Mr. Hamdi. I know what is happening between you and my mother... and frankly, I don't care about her nor am I worried. So let her do what she likes. This is not her first time, and it won't be her last."

Malak's words amazed me despite the difficult situation I was in. I could understand that it might not be the first time that Ingie has had an affair with a man outside of marriage, this even seemed natural and logical in her case. But, what did Malak mean by saying "and it won't be her last?!"

I tried to respond to Malak so as not to prove her accusations with my foolish silence. "My dear Malak. I think you are wrong about..."

"No, Mr. Hamdi. I think you are the one who's wrong. You are wrong to think that my mother loves you, or even likes you, or even cares."

Malak, with her innocent and honest words, was toying with my mind like the stormy winds would play with a small boat. Malak's shocking statements rolled and I gaped, staring at her like a lunatic.

"My mother asked about you before she called you to give me piano lessons. She was reluctant to hire you as my tutor, but the minute she learned from her friends that you were married to the daughter of one of the wealthiest and most influential families, she decided to hire you immediately. Not to be my tutor, but to be her next victim. She decided to cast her nets around you, and to take you from your wife in any way... before she knew you, even before she saw you."

The storm raged inside my head; my thoughts were drowning in each other. This couldn't be right. I couldn't have been taken advantage of twice by two women whose only thing they have in common is my own stupidity and naivety!

"Malak. What you say can't be true..."

"It is the truth and nothing but the truth... This is my mother, Mr. Hamdi... She loves to break women's hearts... She loves to humiliate them and kill their femininity... She snatches their husbands and makes them fall into her love... A love that is not a desire for feelings or even a lust for men... Rather, it is a desire for revenge and retaliation from all womankind."

"Malak, please! your mother is a virtuous lady, and it is not right that..."

"Dear sir, my mother is a whore! Forget this meaningless talk and let's agree on one thing... She is my mother... I love her madly... But she is a whore! This is not our problem or the subject of our discussion, our problem is you!"

"Me... ?!!"

"Yes. You, you are a great artist, Mr. Hamdi, and I have the utmost respect for you, and I hope to continue learning piano on your hands, even if you are in a relationship with my mother... The problem with this relationship is you... you think of yourself as her only lover, while you are just a name in a long list of clients. Clients that my mother decided to wreck the marriages of and destroy their wives."

Malak's words jolted me heavily. Not only because of the way it insulted my manhood, this manhood that I was still trying to regain my faith in, but also for the way and manner in which this poor young lady spoke. What had she seen and heard in this house that would grant her all this sad and woeful wisdom?

"Believe me, Mr. Hamdi. I have seen this list change and change, it gets longer and shorter, it overflows and drains. Since her separation from my father, she has cast her nets on several married men... and the higher the wife in beauty, money, or family, the more valuable the 'hunt' for my mother... and the more the man loves his wife, the more delicious the prey for the 'hunter'.

She deludes every prey to believe that he is her only sin and her sole mistake. She seduces them until they become captives in her bed, until the promised day comes; the day when the poor man comes to her happily saying 'I broke up with my wife! From now on I will be yours alone'. At this moment my mother bares her fangs and shows her claws. She throws the poor man out of her heaven and leaves him to dry his tears and wash his sins, while she celebrates her victory over a new wife."

"... Why, Malak? Why would she behave like that? I can't find a reason..."

"It is my father. That's why. He was totally in love with her, but he was also totally in love with all the women of the world! and as he made love to her, he made love to many of them! He used to treat her like a queen, then betray her with the scums, protect her like a jewel, then wallow with others in the dirt. He showed her that he married her because he adored her, but not because she could satisfy him as a man. So, she woke up one day and has decided to take revenge, not only from my father but rather from all the women of the world."

And again, for the second time that week, I tried to talk. Not because I had anything to say, but just to make sure I was still awake and sane.

"But... Malak, your mother..."

But Malak insisted on going on with her punches and blows. She squared her shoulders and looked me straight in the eyes as she continued.

"Mr. Hamdi. I'll tell you again. I don't care about my mother and what she does, and I think – rather I am almost certain – that her end will be at the hands of one of her lovers who will lose his mind and kill her after she expels him from her paradise, and I am not bothered with this idea. Not because I hate her or wish her death, but because I find this a solution to her pain and an end to her torment and misery. What matters to me is you! I have felt your art and talent since I saw you, and even before I saw you. I heard about you from my friends who study at the Conservatoire. Everyone there praises your talent and your music, and everyone expects you to have a brilliant future in the theaters of London and Paris, and how I hate that this future ends in my mother's bed. Please, don't let the warmth of her bed melt your mind. The day you'll become hers alone will be the last day you'll see me... and I'll see you."

At this moment the door of the house opened and Ingie entered. Malak quickly returned to playing the piano and I quickly put my eyes on her hands while she was playing. We both avoided looking at Ingie so she would not see our faces and realize there was something happening behind her back. Malak returned to play "Confessions"! after she killed me with her confessions.

I didn't talk to Ingie for the whole lesson and didn't even try to look at her, she sat quietly puffing her Nat Sherman cigarettes, reading her magazines, and looking at me! I didn't see her but the flames of her looks were burning through my back all the way to my heart. I was gazing in the hands of Malak playing piano, but I could not hear a single note she was playing. My mind was screaming in rebuff and denial... This was not my life, and this was not my world. This was a boxing match; a boxing match that I was heavily losing!

At the beginning of the week, Ihab hammered me with punches of truth, shattering my dreams of glory, and at the end of the week, Malak surprised me with her knockout to destroy what was left of my dignity and manliness. And there was no towel thrown to end my disgrace, nor was there a ring to save my face.

At this point, I couldn't finish the lesson. I got up and went to the door. Surprised by my sudden action, Ingie looked at me in annoyance and said, "Mr. Hamdi, is there something wrong?"

"I'm sorry, Madame Ingie. I'm sorry, Malak. It's a terrible headache. Excuse me, I have to go."

Ingie got up to escort me to the door, while I looked cautiously and shyly at Malak, who was still sitting in front of the piano, looking at me with a mixture of sadness and pain. I nodded at her and hurriedly left. Ingie tried to talk to me at the door, but I apologized gently and ran out in a hurry.

I left the villa and went off the streets. I kept walking for hours, and kept my face down all the time. Why did I keep it down like that? Was it me feeling ashamed of my stupidity and idiocy? Or was it the punches of all those around me, forcing my head to the ground?

Or was it the remnants of my sanity telling me to stop looking up, chasing a phantom called glory, and start looking down to see where I was going instead?

After hours of walking, the hurricane Malak created began to calm down, and a terrible struggle between certainty and doubt took its place. Malak's words were not devoid of poise and wisdom. However, though her mental age was obviously much higher than her real age, Malak was still too young to realize the complex and intertwined life of adults, and perhaps she saw something on her mother that made her build this exaggeratedly dark image about her behavior, without there being a solid basis for all her suspicions.

Finally, I was home. With no brain to think and no energy to fight, I went to bed with my clothes on, knowing that it would be a long and sleepless night.

So many bad dreams and so little sleep. I was turning in my bed like a wild hog in captivity... Mozart, Chopin, Beethoven, Liszt, Wagner, all these great musicians, and all were looking at me with roaring anger. We have entrusted you as an envoy for our music and a messenger for our arts, and there you were, betraying our trust and chasing your lust. You lost yourself and with it went our faith in you. You neglected your sacred art and hurried after sinful women... You fool! We taught you that the keys to glory were black and white, yet you decided to swing in the swindling area of vicious grayness... You idiot!

Finally, it was morning. I decided to confront Ingie. I would go to her and face her with all the allegations I heard from Malak. I had to know for certain. Am I the love of her heart? Or am I there to keep her bed warm? Or am I just a name in her list of fools?

'La Campanella' played from my phone to stop this shower of questions that I was preparing for Ingie. I looked at the number calling me. It was Ingie's. Great! She saved me the trouble of making the call.

"Baby, I'm calling to check on you. I didn't want to bother you yesterday so I didn't call, I just left you to rest. How are you today?"

"I'm good, Ingie. I will come to you now, there is something I want to talk to you about."

I got no reply from Ingie. I thought the line was cut off.

"Ingie! Are you still there?"

"... You can't come today, my love. I'm busy all morning. Let's talk in the evening, I'll call you at seven."

Ingie hung up, she ended the call in less than a minute and started a fire inside my head. Her hesitation, her excuse not to see me, the way she ended the call, all suggested she didn't want to meet me that morning.

Quickly I put on my clothes and rushed to Ingie's house. I decided to confront her and know what she was up to. I approached the villa, and slowly walked towards the gate. I was working on the things I would tell Ingie; I needed straight answers from her, but at the same time I couldn't expose Malak as the source of my suspicions. As I approached the gate, a muscular young man, with a broad chest and sledgehammers for arms, appeared around the corner, confidently heading towards the gate of the villa as well. I stopped to see where he was going. I found him entering through the gate, but he did not head towards the main door. He veered left in the garden... He was going to... the annex!

I swerved quickly so he would not notice I was heading to the gate as well. I turned around the wall of the villa and hid behind a tree to see who would open for this bastard. He knocked on the annex door confidently.

The door opened... Ingie opened it... in the nightgown... the same slutty nightgown... my nightgown. The bastard couldn't even wait for her to close the door. He squeezed her soft body with his arms and kissed her like an animal. The two went inside... and the door was closed.

My legs could not hold me anymore. I found myself sitting on the sidewalk in front of the villa... like a beggar, a panhandler, begging to understand this world that I never could understand its ups and downs, and scrounging to comprehend those people that I never could realize their cruel behavior. The whole world started spinning and spinning. The whole world was laughing and making fun of me... spinning and revolving... and laughing and giggling. Oh, Ingie, Less than a day has passed since I slept with her, and there she was bringing another mule to make love to her. To this level I was worthless? To this degree I was pathetic? Wasn't there a woman in this whole ugly world who wanted me for who I was and would be satisfied with what I had?! The first one wanted me as a frame to brighten her limited talent, and the second one wanted me as a name to add to her limitless list of sinful lovers... Dina and Ingie... You both deserve to die... You both deserve to be forgotten!

I couldn't get up from the ground, I leaned back against the tree I was hiding behind and I sat there for about an hour. Dark thoughts piled up in my head, shattering the last remnants of my dignity. Why did all the women in my life insist on treating me like I was nothing?! Hanan left me for her new life without bothering to ask about me. Dina deceived me, and deprived me from advancing in my career as a musician, turning me from a talented pianist into a piano teacher. And here was Ingie depriving me of the honor of betraying my wife, and turning me from a secret lover to a client in a brothel.

Damn them all... Damn every woman who thought she could control me with her money or her body... I'd kill you all... I'd burn you... I'd crush you... Let it be the last thing I would do in my miserable life.

Mephisto - Liszt

At this point, I got up. I staggered, not knowing where to go. I went back to my old house, and to my old piano; the piano that my mother had sold her jewelry to buy for me, my old and faithful companion. I put all my anger into playing Liszt's Mephisto. If Dina deserved Bartók's Allegro barbaro, then Ingie definitely deserved Liszt's Mephisto.

I played for hours and hours, and as usual, my mad playing helped me vent my anger and put my thoughts in order. Patience and planning, Hamdi, patience and planning.

* * * *

Two days passed during which I managed to overcome my pain and collect my scattered dignity. I decided to keep things running as they were until I could see how I could make both of these witches pay for destroying my life.

On the time of Malak's piano lesson. I was at the villa on time, I mean, half an hour before time. I went to the annex first to do my homework for Ingie. Was I doing this as part of my scheme of revenge? Or was it to keep my piano lessons with Malak going? Or was it because I became addicted to Ingie's bed like Sayed was addicted to Heroin? I was not sure... All I knew was that I was at the annex... half an hour before the piano lesson.

"Hamdi, I don't like the way you are in! What is wrong with you?!"

Ingie rested her head on her hand as she lay on the bed and covered with the sheet, leaving her alabaster legs uncovered. It seemed that my 'performance' that day was not up to her 'expectations'. So I had to improvise.

"I'm afraid, Ingie. I'm afraid my wife will discover my love for you. The poor woman will go completely crazy if she knows what's going on here."

Ingie's face shone as if she had won a lottery jackpot. Malak was absolutely right in everything she told me about her mother and her lust for women's destruction. This woman took pleasure in deceiving the wives, not in making love to the husbands.

"Do you think she suspects anything?"

"I think she is starting to doubt. Since I met you, I've been avoiding her. I stopped sharing my bed with her. She is definitely oppressed and wounded by this negligence from my side, and she's dying to know the reasons for this change of hearts I'm going through."

"And what will you do?"

"Nothing. I'll just keep loving you."

It seemed that all those lies I came up with and poured in the ears of this lusty homewrecker was much more arousing to her than any foreplay, as she savagely grabbed me back to bed and showered me with kisses and hugs. Nothing could awaken this monster like the news of women's suffering because of her, what a serpent!

Half an hour later I was with Malak for her piano lesson. She didn't ask and I didn't tell. Both of us agreed, silently, to keep everything as is. She would bear the burden of knowing, and I would bear the sin of doing, all for the sake of keeping our piano lessons and the divine fraternity growing between us.

The Abyss

"What could be worse than to live your life waiting for bad news from, about, or because of the people you love."

The lesson was over and I left Ingie's villa. I was planning to get back to my old apartment like I did the last couple of days, but I've decided to head to Dina's house instead. It's been a while since I talked to Sayed, and I wanted to make sure that he was okay. I felt responsible for his poor soul as I felt responsible for Malak and her delicate spirit. I went straight to Radi's room and knocked on the door. The poor man trembled when he saw me at the door.

"Oh, Mr. Hamdi, Has Sayed done anything to disturb you?"

Poor thing! No one came to him except to complain about Sayed. What could be worse than to live your life waiting for bad news from, about, or because of the people you love.

"No, Radi. It's just that I haven't seen Sayed in a while and I wanted to see him."

"Tell me, for God's sake, Mr. Hamdi, please. Did Sayed do something to upset you?"

"No, Radi. He is a friendly and quiet young man, he loves music, and I am spending most of my time alone, so let him come and spend some time with me."

Radi's face shined with a big childish smile and said, "Yes, sir. I will definitely tell him. Sure."

In the evening I found Sayed knocking on the door.

"I'm sorry, Mr. Hamdi, sorry for coming here so late at night. I came as soon as I received your message."

"Never mind, Sayed. How are you?"

I said that as I opened the door to Sayed to let him in. He took a few shy steps to come into the house while saying, "From bad to worse, and I can't complain. It is my path I decided to take till the end. All I hope is for this end to be near."

"You don't live with your father, Sayed. Where do you live then?"

"I do not live with my father because I love him... Addicts like me destroy everyone around them and drag them into the abyss with them, especially the ones they love the most. As for where I live... Well, in the streets, there is always room for people like me in the streets, sir."

I pointed to Sayed to take a seat while asking him, "Do you love your father, Sayed?"

"He's the only thing I love in my life. He's the only right and bright thing in my wrong and dark world. If it wasn't for him, I'd be fast tracking my way down, fearing nothing and missing no one."

"Are you afraid of him?"

"In fact, I fear for him. I have been hearing all my life that his family were tough, hard-headed and thick-skinned. As for my father, he got nothing from them except his dark skin and his white heart; the heart of a poet and the feelings of an artist! He could neither bear my loss nor the shame of my death as an addict, nor does he have anyone else as I am his only son. Yet he never revolts, hits and curses me, or even disavows me, which is torturing me to the bone!

He is like a chain that ties me to the land of humiliation... like a rock that blocks my way to the abyss."

173

I Leaned towards Sayed, looked him in the eyes and said, "But I saw you push him to the ground!"

Sayed looked back at me with eyes full of sadness together with muddiness, and replied slowly.

"It is my insanity when I can't find my Heroin and my agitation when my addiction repossesses my body. I do not hide from my father when I miss a dose... Rather, I deliberately come here so he can see me at the bottom of my despair and the demise of my dignity. Perhaps he would then curse and expel me from his fatherhood, and free me from his chains that bind me to him and to the land of dishonor, letting me fly away in peace."

I put my hand in my pocket and pulled out all the cash I had. I handed them to Sayed and said, "Listen, Sayed. Take this money and find yourself a place to live."

Sayed snatched the money out of my hand like a pang, saying in a stammering voice, "Thank you, sir. And I can assure you that this money will not put a roof over my head as you wish, not even for one week, but it will dwell me in the clouds for a couple of hours."

I totally admired Sayed's brutal honesty. We talked until the early hours of the morning, after which I went into my room and brought a pillow and a blanket.

"Sayed. I will not let you sleep in the street, even if you intend to spend the money I gave you on dope. Take this pillow and blanket and sleep on the stairs in front of the door. I'm sorry, but I can't let you sleep here. You are an addict, and a desperate one. Your addiction may drive you to steal anything or do anything for the sake of the drugs. Dina is traveling, so take your time."

Sayed gave me one of those pure looks of gratitude and said, "Yes, sir... and I thank you."

Sayed went out to sleep in front of the door, and I headed to my room and went to sleep, feeling good about myself for helping this poor soul, even if it was for one night. In the morning I did not find Sayed, I found only the pillow and blanket, I carried them inside and hid them in my room.

* * * *

Around noon I called my 'friend' Hani to confirm the time of our meeting that day. Hani answered, but three hours after my call! We agreed to meet at his house at night. At eight, I was knocking on the door of his apartment.

"Hello, Hamdi, how are you?"

Hani greeted me loudly and warmly as he opened the door wide for me to come in. He continued his talk.

"Frankly, I totally forgot about our date this evening and arranged a party here in the house, but when you called me early this morning I remembered that we're meeting, so I canceled the party, and let the invitees go to hell."

"This is the best thing you have done, Hani. Let our friendship be far from the eyes of people, and from the eyes of Dina."

"Yes, Hamdi. She cannot stand my socializing with other friends without her being present, let alone a friendship with her husband, she will force herself upon us."

Hani's apartment was a nice one. It was obvious that there was a lot of money spent on decorating that place, also it was obvious that there was a lot of goings-on happening in it. That was the typical bachelor pad where all kinds of 'fun' were allowed. We spent time chatting, most of our chat was about the world of Dina. Hani kept joking about how devilish-minded Dina was, telling me what he assumed to be funny stories about the pranks she used to play on others when they were young. And while he saw these pranks as funny and amusing, I saw them as mean and malicious. I could never understand the fun behind hurting others emotionally or physically, except if it was done by psychopaths who see harming others as a source of amusement.

After an hour of talking, Hani went into one of the rooms, then returned after about a quarter of an hour, with a happier face and redder eyes.

"I'm leaving, Hani."

"Hamdi, my friend. No, no way! I am very happy to spend such a nice time with you. I really like you, your personality and your art. Please don't leave."

"No, Hani. It's not my time now; it's the time of your dose of dope, and dope must be respected. It's obvious that you went to your room to sniff your happiness. Now it is running through your veins, reaching your poor head, and taking you high in the sky. I must not be here, or I will pull you back to the ground."

Hani looked at me with gazing eyes and a twisted tongue. I wondered if this was because he was surprised that I knew his secret, or if it was merely the effect of Heroin.

"Does it seem so obvious to you?"

"Hani, if you want to appear as a big addict who is in control of his addiction, then you have succeeded, but if you want to appear as a normal, non-addicted person, then let me tell you that you have failed miserably."

Hani smiled as he scratched his head, and I quickly patted his shoulder as I smiled and said,

"Do not be afraid, my friend. Your secret is well kept with me, though I am sure it is not a secret to anyone who knows you."

I have had enough of Hani for one encounter, so I left with the promise to meet more frequently.

* * * *

Dina returned from her trip. I was so afraid that her surveillance team might have caught my Ingie's 'extracurricular activities' that extended beyond piano lessons, but Dina did not show any sign that she knew about this. I was probably removed from Dina's on-probation list, thanks to my good behavior!

I spent most of my time in my so-called hermitage and she spent hers in her so-called studio. Dina returned haughtier and more arrogant after the 'success' of her 'private' exhibition in London. She has been talking about her expected invitations for world tours, and the possibility of moving to London to be next to her sculpture and fine art 'peers'.

Her lies and deception made me disgusted with her more and more, so I began to make up all kinds of excuses to keep away from her. On her part, she became too busy to worry about me. I started staying in my old house for one or two nights every week, under the pretext that I was rehearsing new pieces of music and I didn't want to disturb her. She began sleeping at her parent's house, claiming she had to run several meetings with the clients interested in her art, and what an art!

For me, Dina turned into a freak like the mutilated freaks that she made in her workshop. She turned into a freak bearing the title of 'wife'. As for the title of 'mistress', it was well deserved by Madame Ingie, whom I no longer dealt with her as a lover or even a whim, but as a prostitute... a prostitute that I pay not with money or presents, but with pity talk and complaints about how far apart I and my wife have become because of her.

I started meeting Hani regularly, we met once a week. He didn't tell Dina about our friendship out of fear of her, and I didn't tell her about this friendship out of contempt for her. Hani began to tell me more and more about his secrets and began to trust me with the details of his life and adventures, and most of his secrets and adventures revolved around the world of women, partying, and addiction.

It was clear from his stories that he tried to be more than a friend to Dina while they were studying together, but she refused and turned him away repeatedly, only because she did not see him worthy of that honor.

It was also clear that Dina played him as she played me, deceived him with the bond of friendship as she deceived me with the ladder of glory, and used him as a tool and a thuggery hand as she used me as a gate and a piano hand.

My relationship with Hani remained the same until that day; the day I found out about Hani and Dina's relationship with the poor soul, Sayed.

"Hani."

"Yes, Hamdi."

"Do you know Sayed?"

"... Sayed who?"

"Sayed was a student with you in college. He was a first-year student when you and Dina were in your senior year."

Hani kept giving me those empty and stoned looks. But I could see that my words hit a nerve in him.

"Don't you know him?! He is the son of the villa keeper; Dina's villa, and he knows you very well."

"Ahh... Sayed. Yes, I know him."

"Tell me, Hani, and please be honest with me. We are friends, and I believe that every human being is free to decide the path he or she will take in their life, and hence I can't blame one person for someone else's choices. So, tell me in all honesty, why did you put Sayed in the path of addiction? His standard of living, background, education, lifestyle... all his traits are totally different from yours, so why did you decide to make him your friend and introduce him to your world of Heroin sniffers?"

Hani hastily stood up and started waving his hands and talking loudly as if she was defending himself in a court of law.

"Hamdi, I didn't do anything. He's the one..."

I interrupted Hani to say with a smile and said, "Oh, my dear. Don't be so defensive. You are a good buddy, no doubt about that. Here I am, your friend for several months now, neither did I ask you to show me the world of addiction, nor did you try to talk me into it, not even as an experiment or to have some fun. So, if Sayed has decided to surrender himself to this path, then this is his business and his choice, not yours."

Hani lowered his head and fiddled with his pack of cigarettes on the table as he said, "I did not and do not wish to harm any human being on the face of this earth. I am a peaceful person, more peaceful than you can imagine, Hamdi. You must've known me by now, I don't think you saw me intentionally hurting anyone... Oh God, except hurting myself of course. You may find me doing evil from time to time, but this is only to maintain my prestige and reputation in this filthy world in which I live, the world of addiction and addicts. But in the end, I am a simple and peaceful human being."

"And Sayed. What is his story?"

Hani shook his head and looked at me steadily, with his arms outstretched as if to deny any accusations I may throw at him, and said, "It was not me who pushed him into this sinister path."

"It was not you who pushed him, but at least you gave him a nudge!"

"No, Hamdi... please... I was just a tool... I had to do what I had to do."

"Do you want to tell me you were forced to tempt Sayed to addiction?! come on."

"Yes, my friend... Yes... It was not me... please believe me... I had to."

"Nonsense! Hani. You wanted to destroy the guy..."

"No! Don't say that... Please... It was not me... It was your wife... Dina!"

The Evil

"Oh, how I hate poverty. It is the synonym of humiliation and indignity, my friend. It is losing every race and winning only the disgrace. It is the constant feeling of guilt even when the truth is on your side."

His words pierced my mind like a bullet to settle in its place in the list of Dina's sins and transgressions. It was only then that I was sure of the thought that stuck in my head when Sayed first told me his story. Now I realized the miserable story and learned another crime of Dina's, but I chose to hear it from Hani, so I turned to him in amazement.

"Dina?! And what does she have to do with this matter?!"

"Dina hated Sayed more than she hated death. This poor man embodied all of Dina's obsessions and fears. He was truly talented and she lacked talent. He was loved by his colleagues and professors and she was deprived of the simplest degrees of acceptance and charisma. She had all the money and all the means, but she could not make even a Matryoshka doll, and he had nothing but dirt and misery but could make legendary art out of that dirt.

Dina was aware of all this, and realized that this miserable one would precede her to the world of art and glory, leaving her to the dumpster of forgetfulness. His name became like a fire eating her heart. Every time this poor person was mentioned, she would shout, curse and slander him with the vilest words. Many of our peers noticed this; they noticed that Dina always lost her usual arrogant calmness and coolness whenever Sayed was mentioned, so they started to take advantage of that to tease her and to drive her crazy. Some even went so far as to tell Sayed about her doings, pushing him to file a complaint with the college administration about the way she talked about him."

Hani leaned back in his seat, threw his hands on the side and stared at the ceiling for seconds. He then continued,

"Until that ugly day ... the day Sayed decided to confront Dina. We were surprised by him approaching her in her clique, and I was one of them. Sayed saluted her, but she did not respond. He asked her why she was always angry with him, and why she was repeatedly talking bad about him. She turned her face away and did not reply. The poor guy started talking to her back, telling her how much he respected her and saw her as a colleague, and that he would expect her to do the same. Dina did not answer or even look at him. The guy could do nothing except turn and walk away. But, this was Dina we are talking about! She would never accept this Sayed 'lecturing' her like he did. So this unjust woman rushed behind him, grabbed him violently by the shoulder to turn him around, then slapped him on the face with all her might."

I wanted to say something. I wanted to curse Dina and curse Hani for being her friend. But there was no way I was going to stop Hani from completing the story, so I kept my mouth shut and continued listening.

"It was an unforgettable scene. We all panicked by what this heartless cruel woman did. Sayed's tears petrified in his eyeballs, he hurried away before his tears betrayed him and everyone saw them running down his cheeks. Some of those who saw what happened moved, not to blame Dina or to calm Sayed, but to inform the administration of what Dina had done attacking a colleague.

But they did not need to do so; The Vice Dean was passing by and saw, himself, everything that had happened. This gentleman was a talented artist and not just a member of the faculty, he had just returned from a mission abroad, and Dina and her behavior represented everything the man rejected and hated in our world, so he insisted on opening a formal investigation, summoning Sayed and most of us to be witnesses."

A bitter smile appeared on Hani's lips as he continued talking, "The investigation began... and it ended five minutes after it began! Poor Sayed denied that he had been slapped or insulted, and insisted that nothing had happened. When the Vice Dean confronted him with what he saw by himself, Sayed insisted on denying everything and mentioning, repeatedly, that he did not submit any complaint. But the Vice Dean, who loved Sayed and admired his talent, did not accept that poor guy being insulted by the tyrant Dina. So he insisted that Sayed should get at least his most basic rights—and if only he didn't. He insisted that Dina should apologize to Sayed... He insisted that she should apologize in his office, and in front of everyone who attended the incident.

This was the worst night in my entire life. Deprive me of my dope for a whole week, but don't take me through this night again or even remind me of it. It was all non-stop crying, screaming, wailing, and endless cursing. All the malice and hatred of the demons against the children of Adam gathered in Dina's heart and then found its way to her tongue, and I was the poor one whom she dragged into her swamp of bitterness and hatred that day.

The next morning, Dina apologized. Her apology to Sayed was as if she were cursing him, and he was standing before her looking humiliated and ashamed as if he was the guilty one. Oh, how I hate poverty ... It is the synonym of humiliation and indignity, my friend. It is losing every race and winning only the disgrace. It is the constant feeling of guilt even when the truth is on your side."

I wanted Hani to stop preaching to me about poverty with all those big words that he was using, and return to this even-more-miserable-than-I-thought story. So I interrupted him to ask, "What about Dina's father? He could've stopped all of this with one phone call."

"Dina's father had had enough of his daughter's nonsense. This is a man who knows how to play the game; he can remove government officials and change a country's policies if he wants, without anyone knowing about him. He always believed that stealth and secrecy are the keys to his success, and his daughter was far from being stealthy or subtle; she was always making mistakes, and she made them with roaring bangs. So that time, her father decided to teach her a lesson by not interfering in the investigation, especially since he loved Radi and saw him as a good man, and liked Sayed and saw him as a great future artist."

"Okay, Hani. What happened next? Go on."

"At night I was surprised by Dina paying me a visit to my house. I was having a little party when she snatched me from my friends and dragged me like a sheep to my room, then pushed me onto my bed. She stood on top of my head, gnashing her teeth in rage and saying, 'Hani. I'll tell your dad about your addiction. I'll make him leave his business abroad and come back to you. I'll make him put you in an addiction sanatorium. There they will hold you a prisoner and treat you like a dog. All your beautiful world I'll destroy for you ...'

'Dina. What is all this nonsense?! What are you talking about?! What do you want?!'

'It's this bloody Sayed... I want him to become a junkie in a week! I want him to be a sniffer, a heavy doper, a drug slave! I want him to be unable to walk or talk, let alone make sculptures! I want him expelled from the college, shunned by the people, doomed by the bricks of the earth.'

'Dina!! What is all of this?!'

'A week, Hani. You have one week. Otherwise, be prepared to go and pick up your father from the airport, and from there you can go directly to the sanatorium.'"

Hani grabbed my arm as if he was begging for forgiveness, and whispered, "Hamdi, this damned woman did not leave me any escape or a way out. The nightmare of any addict is not running out of the dope, the nightmare is the sanatorium. There you are a servile slave, a slave to the dozens and dozens who have understood the game of addiction treatment. They take advantage of you and drain your money and dignity, and even your body. I had no escape, Hamdi... I had to carry out Dina's diabolical orders, regardless how evil they were."

It was all obvious to me now. The diabolical plan of Dina to destroy that poor soul called Sayed. But I wanted Hani to continue talking, and he did.

"I began to get closer to Sayed, I started inviting him to my parties, which for him was a dream that he couldn't even have in his sleep. I began to introduce him to the demons of these parties as a great artist and a talented sculptor. Sayed, the next Mahmoud Mokhtar, the successor of Henry Moore. Vanity began to seep into the heart of the poor man until it took possession of him, then I pushed him to believe that the true artist could not reach the top of his creativity except in the presence of drugs.

I convinced him that heroin would reveal to him new dimensions in his talent that he had not yet traversed, and he would never have realized without it, and the poor thing believed me. He started asking me for a couple of doses to experiment, and his doomed journey began from there."

"In a week, Hani? You destroyed the man's life in a week?"

That idiot answered me as if I was blaming him for pushing Sayed to the dark path of addition too fast!

He said, "The plan took more than a week to complete, but in the end it was done. Dina carried out her infernal plot as she wanted. But... Oh Hamdi, Dina was not satisfied with what she did... rather, she insisted that Sayed's father remain at her service, even when she moved to the villa in which she lives now. She insisted on taking the poor man with her. She was delighted to see Sayed's father serve her and grovel for her to help his useless addicted son... Oh Hamdi, it's when the abundance of wealth and power combined with the lack of conscience and morals... This is us Hamdi. This is my and Dina's world."

"And what a world it is, Hani... What a world!"

"Hamdi. I am not telling you this story to make you hate your wife or resent your life with her. Rather, I was answering your question and absolving myself — even if a little—of Sayed's guilt. Let me also tell you that it all happened a long time ago, and Dina has grown and matured, and she no longer does such things. Not anymore."

Hani continued his worthless defense, trying to soften what he said and justify what he did, and also trying to protect Dina's image in my eyes.

For me, I stopped listening to what he was saying or even hearing his voice. My mind just shut him down. How could my heart deal with all this hatred? How could my soul accept all this malice? And how could this Dina be that vicious? Dina, you cursed brat! Fate has given you everything that a person could desire, and more. Money, influence, family and connections, but you left all that and chased talent, the one and only thing that fate decided not to give you! Why didn't you enjoy what you have? Why didn't you enjoy your money and your life? Why didn't you go around the world,

buy all the gems and the antiques you like, or even build yourself a skyscraper or a spaceship?! Why didn't you do any of this and leave alone those who got nothing but talent? Let them struggle with their gift and run after their dreams, may they find their way to glory.

And if this was the cursed nature of the human soul that runs behind all that is unavailable and seeks to achieve the unattainable, then why the hatred and envy for those with talent? Why try so hard to exclude them and undermine their achievements?! Hey stupid! No one wins the talent race by acclamation... No one wins the talent race by acclamation.

Dragging my feet, I left Hani's house. I kept wondering about what I have done to myself; I was happy in my solidarity, satisfied in my shell, content with my isolation and my devotion to my music. But now, and since I knew that man-eater, I became immersed in her putrid swamp of hatred, drowning in the muds of Ingie's infidelity, sinking in the whirlpool of Sayed and the waves of Hani. Damn you all... and damn the piano lessons.

The Butterfly

"Imagine when your only way to hold to a virtue is

to commit a sin!"

The only good thing that I gained from my piano lessons was Malak... the gentle and meek butterfly, whose tenderness was only exceeded by her sharp mind and clear insight. I was enjoying our side conversations that grew with time. In the beginning, I was taking on the role of her mentor, treating her as my mentee and protégé. But soon I felt that she had the high intelligence and the common sense that qualified her to guide me, especially with all the upheavals and turbulences that I was going through. I started telling her my problems and asking for her opinion and advice. She knew about my relationship with her mother, but she never spoke to me about it again and never asked me to stop. She knew that if this relationship ended, the piano lessons would stop, and we both didn't want that to happen.

In Malak, despite her young age, I found the sister of whom I was deprived. She was younger, more tender and more gentle than my sister Hanan. She was also smarter and much more talented. The main reason I kept my relationship with Ingie was to continue seeing my new sister, Malak, during our piano lessons. Imagine when your only way to hold to a virtue is to commit a sin!

And it was time for Malak's lesson, and as usual, I went half an hour earlier. I headed to the brothel first and then went to the lesson.

The story of poor Sayed and Hani was still burning in my head, so I was distracted and sad during the lesson... and in bed.

Ingie did not care about my distraction and coldness, she became like any prostitute who cared about her fees, and I paid. I told her that my wife confronted me and that she broke down in tears, and that she began to feel that she was not a woman enough to satisfy me. I flooded Ingie's ears with a torrent of lies about my destroyed wife, and she flooded me with love and passion in exchange for these lies. However, my mind was all taken by Sayed and his sad story.

As soon as I finished the lesson and got out of the villa, I found Malak rushing behind me in the garden.

"Mr. Hamdi. What's the matter? I could see you sad and distracted throughout the lesson."

I couldn't tell Malak about Sayed and Hani. She was too young to listen to these horrible stories, so I decided to tell her about my other, and bigger, concern; the one that she knew almost all its details from our previous discussions. I started talking about Dina and her failing me in my career.

"I don't know, Malak, where the path I'm following will take me. My wife has not fulfilled any of her promises to me, and time is passing by. I feel that the flame inside me is fading. I'm turning into a piano tutor knocking on the doors of wealthy clients rather than a piano master knocking on the doors of opera houses all over the world."

"Would you take my advice?"

I looked at her with a smile and said, "Please."

"Face your wife. Face her with the facts. Don't get angry or lose your temper. Just remind her of what happened between you two in your first meetings. You didn't love each other, and neither of you showed affection for the other. There was a clear agreement between you, a fully-fledged deal; you would be her husband, and she would be your access to those who control matters in the world of music. You obviously fulfilled your part in this deal, so where is her part?"

"I've spoken to her before."

"Yes, you have spoken to her before, but it is evident that you spoke timidly as if you were asking her for a favor or a loan. You had a deal with her, and now you are claiming your share of the profits this deal brought, and this is your right indeed."

"But what's the use of all of this?! I told you before; this woman called Hans to stop me from joining his school. So how come she will turn around and help me now?!"

"Yes, she called Hans, but she thinks that you don't know that. And this gives you all the right to ask her—with all the naivety and innocence in the world—to talk to Hans, and to whoever can help you. Insist on your position and push her to make the calls. She may bend under your pressure and fulfill her part, and then you live happily ever after, or she will refuse, which will reveal her bad intentions about your future. This allows you to get back to your path and take matters into your own hands, and in both cases, you are the winner.

Otherwise, she will keep procrastinating, and you will remain passively disappointed and frustrated, and you will achieve nothing."

"I don't know Malak. What you are saying totally and absolutely makes sense. It's just that I'm..."

"Mr. Hamdi, You were raised on the concepts of right and wrong, virtue or vice. You were taught that life is like the keys of a piano; they are either white or black. There are no gray keys in a piano, but life has a huge and vast gray area, an area that you don't know and never experienced. That's why you don't know how to move or maneuver in it, while others know and understand these gray keys like the back of their hand."

Malak's words were so deep and praiseworthy that I found myself forgetting all about my problems and thinking only about her. How could a young girl like her possess all this wisdom and prudence?! It must be the only benefit of living in a house full of tragic incidents like Ingie's.

"How beautiful you are, Malak. How I wish I had your wit and sanity."

"Sir, you are so smart... smarter than you think.

The whole story is that the one standing outside the whirlpool of events sees things more clearly and objectively, unlike the one who is immersed in its core, and who feels too overwhelmed to think properly."

Malak looked at me with a sad look in which pain was mixed with hope, then she continued her words in a voice overpowered by melancholy, "I really hope that things go like you wish and that you reach the fame and glory that you definitely deserve, even if this means that I lose my tutor and my source of inspiration."

Malak turned her face so that I could not see her tears, and hurried home. Oh, Malak... a butterfly made of silk, with a mind made of gold, and a mother made of filth.

I took my time getting back to Dina's villa, I was trying to prepare what I was about to tell her. It was the confrontation I wished I wouldn't have to face, and I had to be ready to state my case clearly, and deal with all her angry and insulting responses in a wiser manner.

I gave myself no opportunity to back off or to hesitate, and as soon as I saw Dina before me, I started the talk, "Dina. We need to talk."

Dina gave me one of her cold and careless looks and said slowly, "Go ahead."

"We have been married for about a year, and during this period I have tried to be a good and obedient husband as much as I could, and I think that I have fulfilled all my duties as a husband."

Dina continued with her cold and careless look, although I could see that she was getting ready for the fight, but that didn't stop me from going ahead with my talk.

"However, after a whole year, I'm still the same. No contact with your acquaintances in the world of music, No musical performances, No meetings with producers, No negotiations for a contract, not even an invitation from a school for talented musicians. Indeed, I can even say without any doubt that during this whole year I have not seen a single musician that you were the reason I got to know."

"I told you, Hamdi. These things need planning, and building your image as a talented artist needs time and effort. So let me do my work calmly and thoughtfully."

"Dina, I don't need you or anyone to build me an image or brand my talent as you say! Just put me with those music producers and a piano in the same room, and let me play my music and let them be the judges. I don't need publicity to highlight my talent. I just need to meet those in charge. So, please, arrange this meeting and leave the matter to me."

Dina stood up vigorously as if she was going to attack me, and yelled, "Hamdi, your words carry a lot of arrogance! Who told you that you are that good?! Who told you that you are ready for the world of professional musicians?!"

I jumped in before she continued insulting me.

"I know my capabilities and I weigh my talent very well, Dina, and when I met Hans..."

Dina interrupted me, in turn, screaming, "Hans?! Hans doesn't want you! He refused to invite you to his school, and I tried over and over again to convince him, but he refused."

You wicked! You lying and evil woman! How dare you! Twisting the facts and throwing lies with a straight face. I shouted back with all my anger and frustrations,

"This is not true! You know that this is not true."

"Are you calling me a liar?! Well, did you talk to Hans and ask him? Who did you talk to? Tell me... Who spoke to Hans and told you otherwise?"

The cursed bitch! She called me a talentless musician and then asked me to prove the opposite. She turned the argument so cunningly that it became about who had spoken to Hans and who had told me he wanted me at his school. Even if I told her that it was Ihab, this bastard would not support me; he would probably crumble and hide to protect his family's business. He has already disappeared and there was no news about him. As for Hans, he would not sacrifice one of his most important sponsors and supporters for my sake.

I had to drag her back to the topic at hand, which is to explain her reluctance in making these calls to her so-called friends and relatives in the world of music.

"Dina, listen..."

"No! You listen, Hamdi. This is all I have for you, and my advice to you is to work harder to improve your skills, and then I will try to find someone who is willing to help you. But if you continue to be engulfed by your arrogance and surrender to the delusion of talent that you claim, then it's better for you to spend your life as a piano teacher."

"I... I claim talent... Oh, you..."

"NOOOOOO."

This loud, anguished and horrible "no" did not come from me, nor from Dina. Rather, it came from the ground floor of the villa. I opened the door and quickly went downstairs, and Dina came behind me.

The screaming rose again, though this time it was rattled and full of tears. The scream was coming from Radi's room. I quickly rushed into the room, only to find Sayed on his knees, embracing his father's head who was lying on the floor, and shouting in a tearful and broken sound.

"No... don't leave me... don't leave me... Dad... don't leave me alone... I have no one but you... Dad... Oh, God... Oh, God... Every day I pray for you... I pray to die... every day... a thousand times... a thousand times I pray... But here you are... keeping me ... and taking my father ... This is supposed to be my turn... not his... I have more right to die than him... I am more deserving of death than him... Oh, God... Oh, God."

I found myself on my knees, hugging Sayed.

I hugged him as I hugged my brother Hassan on the bathroom floor years ago. I grappled with the Angel of Death before to keep him away from Hassan, to leave him for me, and I failed... and there I was grappling with him so he would keep away from Sayed and be satisfied with the soul of his father.

Radi has died. The only thing that was pure in this damned and wicked place has died. Don't be sad, Sayed. The chain that held you to the land of humiliation is gone, and the rock that blocks your way to your Abyss is gone. So, fly towards the chasm if you want or dare.

The workers in the neighboring buildings started to gather after hearing Sayed's screams and cries. They tried to release Radi's body out of Sayed's hands, and they barely managed to do that after a long struggle. Sayed gave in at last, leaving his father's body, and threw himself in my arms, sobbing.

Some people started carrying the body of Radi to his bed, while others hurried to prepare whatever was necessary in such cases, and Sayed was still in my arms crying incessantly. And in the midst of all that, I heard Dina talking over her phone, "Hello Mama. This housekeeper, Radi, has died. I can't stand it here.

I'm gonna come and stay with you for a few weeks."

It was Sayed's arms wrapped around my shoulders and clinging to me that stopped me from pouncing on her and smashing her head. She didn't even bother to make that call away from this poor fellow. How can anyone be so mean and spiteful? How can indifference reach this abhorrent degree?!

I unloaded my anger and frustration into the arms of Sayed. We both cried and sobbed like children snatched from our mothers' arms. We cried until everyone around us cried as well.

The repentance

"My calf was my fall into the abyss of addiction… while your calf was your submission to anything but your talent… So repent to your creator, my friend… repent to your creator."

The preparation for the burial ended in the morning, and we went to accompany Radi's body to its final resting place. Sayed disappeared immediately after the burial. I searched everywhere but couldn't find him. I decided not to go back to the villa; I went back to my old house. I sat in front of my old piano and played the Lacrimosa. I played the Lacrimosa on the day of Hassan's death, and on the day of my mother's death... and here I was playing it for Radi. Even my father did not get the honor of the Lacrimosa.

But, only minutes had passed when heavy knocks on the door interrupted my Lacrimosa. I wondered who would come knocking on my door at this late hour of the night? Nobody knew I was here. I opened the door, anxious to see who my visitor was. It was Sayed!

"Sayed! Come in. How did you know about this address?"

"From the letters you used to get in the villa, on some of them there was your old address."

"Come in, Sayed. come."

Sayed was in a pitiful state. His drooling mouth and his cloudy eyes indicated that his blood carried more dope than ever before.

Sayed walked into the house lumbering, hurriedly crouching on the ground, as if afraid that his feet would not carry him to the nearest seat. He leaned his head against the wall and closed his eyes, letting his drool run down all the way to his chest. More than a quarter of an hour passed and Sayed hadn't moved an inch, I thought he fell asleep... or died. Finally, he spoke.

"Do you know where I was today? Do you know where I went after my father was buried?"

"Where have you been, Sayed?"

"I went to Hani's place. I waited for him to come out, so I could kill him."

My brain shuttered and my body shivered as if I was electrocuted.

"Have you gone mad, Sayed?"

"Don't be afraid, sir. I waited until I saw him coming home. He was alone and I could have easily killed him, but I didn't. I went to him servilely, and I begged him to give me some heroin instead of him begging me to keep his life. He bestowed upon me a generous amount of dope when he learned about my father's death... an amount that put me in the state I'm in now."

"Sayed, don't you ever do that again."

"Why not?! The only thing that stopped me from killing this bastard earlier was my poor father. I was afraid... I was afraid that they would hurt him if I tried to harm this Hani... and now my father is dead, resting in the belly of the earth... and I think it's time for Hani to join him, although I'm sure they will have different paths in the afterlife. Perhaps my father died in order to let me face this bastard and kill him as he killed me and killed the dreams of my poor old man, and if today I got spineless and cowardly and retreated under the lust for the drug, tomorrow I would kill this immoral beast under the ecstasy of the same drug."

"Don't do that, Sayed! This poor Hani... He's helpless like me and you... He was just a tool. He didn't want to hurt you at all... It wasn't him ..."

My words awakened what was left of Sayed's drenched mind, so he opened his eyes and looked at me, saying, "What do you mean?"

I remained silent and did not respond. I did not want to implicate Sayed or to add to his problems, but at the same time, I was tired of the shocks and frustrations crouching on my chest and burning my heart.

"It was my wife... Dina!"

Sayed pounced on my feet, grabbing them while talking to me in a hissing voice, "What do you mean it was Dina?!"

I started telling Sayed, telling him everything... My meeting with Hans. My meeting with Dina. Her promises to pave my way to glory. My decision to accept her marriage proposal. Her breaking the promises she made and accusing me of poor talent... and Hani!

I told him about Hani and Dina, and the plan that Dina set and forced Hani to implement. I told him about her threatening Hani if he didn't obey her orders... I told Sayed everything!

I got it all off my chest, everything... and then sat there waiting for the storm of anger to hit Sayed and to blow me away... but the strange thing was that Sayed did not rebel, nor did he get angry. Instead, he remained silent and calm throughout my talk, even as I told him of Dina's despicable plan to throw him into the abyss of addiction.

He did not try to interrupt me or to stop me, but waited until I finished and then said calmly, "You and I... You and I... indeed we have wronged ourselves by taking the calf for worship... My calf was my fall into the abyss of addiction... while your calf was your submission to anything but your talent... So repent to your creator, my friend... repent to your creator... repent to your creator..."

Sayed kept repeating those last couple of words on his way to the door that he opened quickly, and went away.

I thought I'd rest when I told the whole story to Sayed and got it off my chest, but that did not happen. On the contrary, my chest got tighter till I couldn't breathe, and my mind became dreary till I couldn't think. I took a sleeping pill and forced myself into a disturbed and ill sleep.

* * * *

I woke up early in the morning to heavy knocks on the door. Had Sayed come back again? No, these insanely aggressive knocks couldn't have come from Sayed's hand. I fearfully wondered who was paying me a visit this early in the morning.

My curiosity to know who was knocking overcame my fear of the continuous and disturbing knocks. I rushed to open the door. I was stunned by two raging bulls in the form of human beings storming the house, and behind them, there were four others, no different from them in size and ferocity.

"Police!"

I quickly retreated and pressed my back against the wall so that these raging bulls would not run over me. The six broke into the rooms of the house searching them, while a younger man, who carried the same features of seriousness and sternness but with more calmness and civility, turned to me and said, "Mr. Hamdi."

"Yes."

"I am Major Nazmi Salameh from the General Investigations Department. I have a search and seize warrant under your name. So please come with me, I need to bring you in."

"Seizing who? And bring to where?"

"A seize and summons order in your name, so I will take you now for the General Prosecutor office for questioning."

Major Nazmi was generous enough to repeat himself to me. It was obvious that he was a man of so much strictness and so little patience, but the strange look that I threw at him must've been the reason for him tolerating me; it was a look that mixed horror and confusion with sleepiness from the effect of the sleeping pill I took last night. I gathered all my powers and all my courage just to open up my mouth and say, "Why all of this?!"

"Don't worry Mr. Hamdi, all will be alright, I'm sure. I just need your full cooperation. Is there anyone at this house with you?"

"No, sir."

"Did anyone sleep in this house yesterday other than you?"

"No, sir."

"Who was the last person you saw yesterday?"

"There was a person with me called Sayed; Sayed Radi. He spent about an hour with me and then left at about midnight."

Major Nazmi's features changed, becoming even more serious than before, and he started staring at me so hard that I thought he was going to kill me. However, I still had the courage to ask, "What happened? Please tell me."

He replied calmly while still staring at me, "Sorry. My job is to bring you immediately to the General Prosecutor office. You can change your clothes, but quickly, please."

I didn't move. I waited until the six huge men had finished their search and then went into my room to change my clothes. I was at a total loss. I didn't know what to do or what to say. My brain got too petrified and appalled to think.

From the room I heard the men's feet as they left the house, then I heard the sound of piano chimes. There were fingers trying to play the music of the song 'Ana La Habibi' by the beautiful Fairuz and the legendary the Rahbanis. It is a beautiful song, but those fingers trying to play the melody were like little hammers! They fell on the keys of the piano as if to extract a confession from them, rather than extracting notes and music. This hand was created for many useful purposes, but playing the piano was definitely not one of them.

I hurried out to find Major Nazmi standing by the piano, he was the culprit!

"Hamdi, Do you know how to play the piano?"

"Yes, a little."

"Do you know that song I was playing?"

I hastened to hide the sarcasm that began to rise on my face, despite all the horror I felt... 'You played it' you said?! Better to say you 'hit it'!

"Yes, sir."

"Can you play it for me?"

Ana Le Habiby - Fairouz - The Rahbannis

I sat in front of the piano and started playing, after about a minute I stopped. I was afraid that Major Nazmi would get bored of my playing and would grab me from the neck and drag me out to the police car, but I was surprised when I looked at him to find him enjoying the music so much! His stern features had changed to become calmer and more intimate.

He looked at me and said, with a smile, "I love music, and I was going to be a musician like you one day, but my dad wanted me to become a police officer. My whole family is made of police officers."

Major Nazmi stopped talking and looked at me closely as if he was checking me, then grabbed his radio and ordered the police force accompanying him to leave. He looked back at me and said, "Hamdi, I have commanded the force to leave. You and I shall leave the house but in a little while, without any fuss and without cuffs on your wrists. It will look like we're leaving your house as friends, and this police campaign that came and left had nothing to do with you. I am trying to keep from looking bad in front of your neighbors, and all I ask of you is that you do not try to do anything reckless."

I hastened to interrupt him.

"Excuse me, sir. I am a musician, the most reckless thing I can do is to play crescendos late at night! If this piano resists you or tries to escape, I will too!"

Major Nazmi smiled and said, "Wonderful! Now play something else for me."

"What do you like to listen to?"

"There was a piece of music played in an old series I used to watch. I loved this music and this series very much, but I don't remember its name.

It was a series about two lovers who drifted apart and then met again by chance after a lifetime. I think it was from..."

I rushed to interrupt him before he went on with his memories.

"The Second Encounter. It's called 'The Second Encounter' series. The music is composed by the great Omar Khairat."

The Second Encounter - Omar Khairat

𝄞 221 𝄞

"Uh. Wonderful! Can you play it?"

I started playing. It's absolutely great music, but the most amazing thing was the state of harmony and enjoyment that Major Nazmi went into, and his childishly enthusiastic interaction with the music.

I finished playing, so I stood up, announcing the end of the melody and the end of me playing piano today. Curiosity was killing me to know what was happening so I couldn't waste more time. I was dying to know what the police wanted from me, and why did they search my house?

The features of strictness and seriousness returned to the face of Major Nazmi as if his love for music was a sin that he should've hidden and a defect he should've covered. We got out of the house, went to his car, got in it, and drove off.

"Sir. Will you not tell me what is happening and why I have been arrested?"

"Mr. Hamdi. You are not arrested. You are required for questioning as a part of an investigation run by the prosecution office, and what happened in the search of your home was ordered by the prosecution office, and if our method disturbed you or frightened you a little, please accept my apology."

"Sir, I just want to know what the matter is."

Major Nazmi kept silent and did not reply. After a minute, he came back to speak, "I can't tell you anything, it's up to the general prosecutor to explain things for you. All I can tell you is that you'll meet with the Public Prosecutor, Mr. Khaled Hassan."

I didn't talk. I just waited for him to continue talking. I needed to learn anything from him that could help me figure out what was happening, but Major Nazmi kept quiet.

A few minutes later he looked at me and said, "Hamdi. Will you accept a piece of advice from me?"

"Sir, of course. please tell me."

"Mr. Khaled, the Public Prosecutor, is a man of great intelligence and long experience, and this case is extremely sensitive and crucially important, and all the capabilities of the Ministry are harnessed to solve it. My advice to you is to be honest and straightforward with Mr. Khaled. Don't try to hide anything from him. Answer all his questions with utmost honesty, accuracy, and clarity. If you lie to him once, you will lose him forever, which is not in your best interest."

Major Nazmi's advice added more fears to the ones already eating my brain! For God's sake, what has happened that made the whole Ministry of Interior and justice interested in me?

* * * *

We arrived at the Public Prosecutor Office, and in minutes we were in front of Mr. Khaled, who started his official investigation and questioning immediately, "Mr. Hamdi. Do you know why you are here?"

"No, sir."

"There has been a murder."

The world started spinning around me... This is not a room... This is the Titanic sinking and taking me with it to the bottom... I used to think that life's shocks and blows had made me stronger and that I was no longer easily affected by such calamities, but here I am collapsing before the word 'kill' like any sensitive pianist.

"Who?!! Who was killed?!"

"Your wife... Madame Dina!"

The Incitement

"Have I failed in my career and in my marriage because I thought the ladder to glory would be like the music sheets whose steps were steady and staves were clear, while the rest of mankind hopped on the ladders of their ambitions between shaky steps and faded ridges as the mountain goats do?"

The room was spinning... spinning... the Titanic was sinking... and I was drowning with it... the office... Khaled... the prosecution clerk... everything was spinning... and Dina... Dina... suddenly I remembered nothing but her sweet madness... her beautiful laughter... the way she threw herself in my arms on our wedding day... the musical notes she gave me... I could only remember the few sweet moments we lived together... the damned Dina is gone... only Dina, my wife, remained.

The next thing I felt was a cup of cold water sticking to my lips, and drops of water splashing on my face; it seemed that I lost consciousness for a moment. I looked around and found Mr. Khaled and others gathered around me.

Mr. Khaled returned to sit behind his desk and said, "I'm sorry to inform you of this sad news here and in this way."

"What?! What happened? How...?"

"Mr. Hamdi. Murder investigations have a different style and a special way of handling, and you certainly understand the sensitivity of this particular crime. Madame Dina's family are so sensitive about what has happened to their daughter, and their one and only request is to keep the name of their daughter away from the gossips and bad media, and I think this must be your demand as well, because the victim is your wife, and you certainly want to protect her name."

I looked at him in anger and said out loud, "These people are something else! Shouldn't their main request be the arrest of their daughter's murderer?"

Mr. Khaled ignored my question and my tone of voice, and went on with his official interrogation.

"Mr. Hamdi, I want you to describe to me your day yesterday, minute by minute, and don't leave out any of the details."

I began by recounting the details of my day, and what a difficult day it was! The death of Radi, the burial procedures, Sayed's visit. I told Khaled all the details, but I did not tell him the details of the heated discussion between me and Dina the night before, nor the details of my conversation with Sayed when he came to visit me. I tried to hide anything that indicated my disagreement with Dina or my hatred for her. The last thing I needed was an accusing finger to point at me, implicating me in this heinous crime.

"Mr. Hamdi. Let me ask you. Do you regularly host Sayed in your house?"

"This was the first time he visited me at my old address, but he used to visit me and spend a little time with me in the villa."

"Are you used to spending your time with a heroin addict?"

"Sayed was a simple, peaceful human being pushed by fate into the abyss of addiction. He did not harm me in any way, he loved classical music and loved listening to me playing the piano. He only needed a friend to talk to, and I was that friend."

"Have you ever given him money or valuables?"

"I gave him money several times, but I would give it to him so he can buy food or to find a place to stay, not to buy drugs."

"And what was Madame Dina's opinion of you sheltering and assisting Sayed?"

"Dina didn't know anything about it. She was occupied with her galleries and her parties, and she knew nothing about the visits of Sayed, and I did not want to bother her with such a trivial matter."

"Mr. Hamdi, sheltering and helping an addict with accommodation and money is not a trivial matter. Usually, sympathetic esteemed people like you are the first victims of addicts like him."

"All I know is that Sayed is a kind and gentle person who isn't inclined to violence. His father's work in the service of the villa also made him extra careful in his visits, so as not to harm his father or cause him any embarrassment."

"How did Sayed know your old address?"

"I asked him the same question, and he told me that it was written on some of the letters which I received in the villa, and which he would see when he came to visit his father."

"This means that he was reading your letters and opening them! Did you not have any doubts when he told you this?"

"He read the address on the outer envelope and didn't open any letters."

"Did Sayed use Heroin in front of you?"

"No. It did not happen, and if it did, I would have kicked him out at once."

"Tell me about your brother Hassan..."

His question hit me like the sting of a poisonous scorpion, and so I couldn't help but shout,

"I do not like to include my brother's name in any discussion, even between friends. So how about talking about him with a prosecutor? And what does this bloody investigation have to do with my brother?"

"Calm down, Mr. Hamdi, and carefully watch what you are saying. You are in the Public Prosecution Office, and in an official interrogation..."

"Even if we were in the courtroom, or even if it was Judgment Day! I don't give a damn. My brother Hassan passed away... He died... He died many years ago. You want to know more about him? Want to know the causes of his death and what prompted him to commit suicide? Go to him and ask him!"

Khaled's eyes opened wide in astonishment at my boldness and rudeness. While I came back to say, "I think it is now clear to me. Dina was killed, and you think that I am the killer, and you'll use your provocative methods to get a confession from me. Please, no need for that; I didn't kill Dina, not because I love her or hate her, but because I don't know how to kill an ant."

Khaled leaned back in his seat and looked at me for a long time as if he was peeking into my brain, then he leaned towards me and said,

"Mr. Hamdi, we know very well that you did not kill your wife. We know that because Sayed is the one who killed her!"

The world around me started spinning again... I grasped my seat with both my hands trying to keep my balance... I should've seen this coming... I should've seen this coming... Poor Sayed! He fulfilled his promise to wipe out those who pushed him into the abyss of addiction, but instead of killing the executing hand, he killed the mastermind... thanks to my great guidance and meticulous instructions! Oh my God... What have I done?!

Khaled kept talking, but I could hardly hear a word of what he was saying, "All we want to know are the names of his associates who helped him commit this crime."

I gathered up the rest of my courage and said, "Then, ask him! Interrogate him, perhaps he will tell you about his partners... if he has any partners in the first place!"

I said that to Mr. Khaled with all my remaining strength and courage, while inside I was shivering like a rabbit on a cold night. If they asked Sayed, he would tell them about what I told him yesterday, and I would become an accomplice with him in his crime by incitement.

But Mr. Khaled did me a great favor... a favor that I wished I hadn't gotten.

"Sayed is dead!"

The world revolved around me again, but this time I recovered quickly. I felt relieved that Sayed had died and that my name had not been involved in this crime, I also felt the lowness and guilt of the relief I felt at the death of this poor man.

Mr. Khaled sat straight in his seat, opened the file in front of him, and began reading, "At two o'clock in the morning, while Madame Dina was returning to her father's house, and as she was leaving the car in the garden, the culprit Sayed Radi pounced on her and hit her on the head with a hammer. We are waiting for the forensics report, but it is expected that the victim died with the first blow, or at least she lost consciousness. Sayed continued using the hammer to smash the victim's head, and he also started shouting. His voice alerted the security of the villa, who arrived at the crime scene and saw what Sayed was doing, so they shot him with their licensed pistols, killing him on the spot."

I didn't say a word... I was busy imagining the crime and its ugliness... Poor Dina with her little head smashed by Sayed and his raging hammer... Sayed screaming not in celebration of revenge or in the desire for fame, but for the guards' bullets to come and relieve him of his life... A murdered and a murderer, both of them are dead, and both are victims... one of them was victimized by the abundance of his talent and the scarcity of his means, and the other was victimized by the mediocrity of her talent despite all her power and means.

Mr. Khaled interrupted the gloomy and dark picture I was painting in my head.

"The presence of a relationship in the form of a friendship between you and the perpetrator, and the fact that you were the last person he met and spoke to before he committed his crime, together with the results of our preliminary investigations that indicate the presence of significant disagreements between you and Madame Dina, all these facts make the general prosecution office interested in further investigating if you had a role in this crime. So, we, Khaled Hassan—the first prosecutor, have decided to hold you for four days in custody until the end of the investigation."

I felt like someone had ripped my heart out of my chest and was squeezing all my blood out of it... I am now accused and under investigation... investigation... accusation... trial... and imprisonment. I did nothing, I'm innocent... innocent... Ah, Dina... in your life, you deprived me of my glory, and in your death, you deprived me of my freedom.

I realized that I needed a lawyer to get me out of this catastrophe, but I didn't know anyone. I thought of asking my piano students, their families might recommend good lawyers who can handle my case. But by doing so, I was exposing myself and smearing my reputation with my own hands.

I woke up from my thoughts to Khaled's voice talking to the clerk, "End the record and finish your report, Hussein."

Khaled left his seat and grabbed my arm, leading me to an adjacent room, he let me in and entered with me then closed the door. He pointed to one of the chairs for me to sit down, he sat in front of me, looked me in the eyes, and said in a calm and low voice, "Listen, Hamdi. This is a precautionary measure, and it is more to your advantage than it is to your harm. If you hire any lawyer now, he'll be able to get you out right away, because all the evidence relating to you that exists so far is circumstantial evidence that does not rise to presumption. But believe me, holding you here is in your favor. You will remain in this room. You will not go to pretrial detention with criminals and thugs, your place is not with these mobs. Consider yourself my guest, and all your requests will be answered until this investigation is over."

I didn't know what to say to him. Blows were pouring down on my head and did not give me a chance to think. Mr. Khaled took out his pack of cigarettes and offered me one. I indicated to him that I didn't smoke, he laughed a little and then said,

"Oh dear, I spent enough money on this cursed habit to buy a new house."

I smiled and did not answer. A little while later, someone came carrying food, Khaled invited me to eat with him, I took a few bites and couldn't eat more, but I took a bottle of water and drank it all at once.

Khaled spent about an hour with me, he was a simple and nice man, unlike what he seemed to be in the interrogation room. He started talking to me about music and musicians, as much as his intelligence and perceptiveness in conducting the investigation, he was totally ignorant when it came to music.

"Mr. Hamdi. Was there not a great musician who was deaf yet composed great music? I think it was Bach. Right?"

"No, sir. It was Beethoven. Beethoven was deaf for a long part of his life; he had problems in hearing that gradually progressed until he became completely deaf."

"Wow! Was he really composing his music while he was deaf?!"

"Yes. Indeed, he composed his greatest works while he was deaf, like the Ninth Symphony and 'Missa Solemnis'."

"How did he compose music when he couldn't hear it?"

"He knew every key of the musical instruments, he perceived and memorized each sound they made, and he knew in advance the tones that would come from these instruments according to what he had written in his musical notes. Music was in his heart, mind and soul, not just in his ears."

"So deafness, like blindness, does not prevent a talented artist from being creative?"

"Actually, sir, Bach —whose name you mentioned earlier— spent a part of his life blind, and yet he composed many genius pieces of music, and Handel was also blind, and this didn't stop him from becoming one of the greatest music composers in history. The strange thing is that both of them lost their sense of sight at the hands of the same ophthalmologist."

Khaled got up from his seat while laughing loudly, then said, "If I had been the investigator at that time, I would have put this doctor in prison for life. See you tomorrow."

Khaled left the room and left me alone. Instead of thinking about the predicament I was in and trying to find a solution to it, I found myself going through my entire life... like a movie playing in front of my eyes. I remembered the moments of my joy and the days of my sadness, the flashes of my brilliance and the darkness of my failure. I remembered my father, my mother, Hanan and Hassan. I remembered my first piano lesson with my mom. I remembered the tempo, the halftone, the scale. I remembered all the basic principles she taught me and how beautiful she was.

At that moment, I realized that music was a blessing to its listener and a curse to its player. The listener could taste what he or she heard and imagine in it any way they liked; there were no rules or restrictions for understanding music and reacting to it. As for the poor musicians, they were bound by rules and boundaries they could only move within; rules like the notes and the tempo, the clefs and the staves, the octaves and the keys. Was that why I failed in my life? Because I was looking for rules and regulations in a world without rules or regulations, a world without rhythm or staves, unlike my well-ordered, strictly-organized world of music? Was that why I failed in my life? Because I thought everything will be in black and white, like the piano keys that I've been living with since my childhood, while everyone around me was swaying in gray? Have I failed in my career and in my marriage because I thought the ladder to glory would be like the music sheets whose steps were steady and staves were clear, while the rest of mankind hopped on the ladders of their ambitions between shaky steps and faded ridges as the mountain goats do? Or was it all due to my bad luck and my lack of resources and resourcefulness?

I fell on the old and only sofa in the room trying to sleep. I knew that sleeping in such conditions and on such a sofa was impossible, but what could I do in this deaf, hollow room but try to sleep? Oh, I wish...

* * * *

"Mr. Hamdi... Mr. Hamdi."

I slowly opened my eyes... My eyelids were heavy, I couldn't open them... I didn't know where I was or who was around me.

"It's been over twenty-four hours since you went to sleep! Man! You're one heavy sleeper, we couldn't wake you up."

What was he talking about?! I'm a 'heavy sleeper' he said! I've always suffered from bad and disturbed sleep since I was young. But from the looks on his face and the faces of those in the room it seemed that he was right. I didn't know what happened. How did I sleep all day in such a place and in such circumstances?! I closed my eyes and opened them again as if I was trying to reset my mind. All the men in the room left except for Khaled.

He sat next to me, lit his cigarette and quietly puffed out its smoke, saying, "I need to talk to you. Let's have coffee together and talk."

I went to the bathroom next to his office to wash my face and remove this heavy sleep that overwhelmed me. I came back to the room to find the coffee on the table and Khaled waiting for me smiling.

"Sit down, Mr. Hamdi."

I sat down, quickly grabbed the cup of coffee in front of me, and started sipping it hoping that it might wake me up from my grogginess. Khaled continued smoking his cigarette as he stared at me until I finished my coffee.

"Would you like another cup of coffee?"

"Please, that would be great."

Khaled smiled while looking at me, then ordered the guard to bring us more coffee, he came back to look at me and then said, "Are you ready to talk now?"

"Yes. I think."

"As you can see, this is a friendly conversation. There is no investigative clerk and no recordings, I am just chatting with you. However, I can take you to the interrogation room at any moment and come back to the official investigation based on what you say now. Agree?"

"Agree."

"I have summoned many of Dina's acquaintances to interrogate them and hear their testimonies."

All the sleepiness that clouded my mind vanished. I had a bad feeling about where this was going. Khaled continued, "And among those I summoned and interrogated, was Hani!"

"Hani?!"

"I liked him, he is an excellent young man, and extremely cooperative. All he cares about in life is that his father knows nothing about his addiction.

The problem is that the whole world knows he is an addict! If his father browsed any of his son's pages on social media, he would know right away that his son is an addict. Anyway, Hani spoke to me. He talked... a lot! He told me about the dirty game he played on Sayed, and how Dina forced him to fulfill his role in this diabolical game. I have my own opinion in the matter of addiction in general; my experience taught me not to blame anyone for falling into the abyss of addiction except for the addict himself.

In my experience, no one ever forces the addict to fall into the traps of the abuse except for his stupidity and frivolity, and nothing else. However, I can see that Sayed was a special case. It was a despicable plan by Dina and Hani to set up this poor man and destroy his future and his life."

I didn't know what to say. So I kept my mouth shut, waiting for Khaled to throw the bomb in my face, and he did.

"Hani also told me that he told you the whole story a few days before the crime."

My heart was in my mouth... Khaled knew it all... He knew it all... He knew then that I had a way to pressure Sayed and chirp in his ears to kill my wife.

Khaled stopped more of the dark thoughts from pouring into my poor brain when he said,

"The scenario that I see now is the following: There was a great disagreement between you and your wife, there was a strange relationship between you and her addicted killer, and there was great harm that was inflicted on the killer by the victim. All that was needed was for you to connect the dots, and you did! This means that you were not the killer, but you were the instigator. What do you think?"

At this moment, I could not remain silent. There was no point of hiding anything from the man. I talked, but this time I told Khaled everything. The first time I talked openly was with Sayed when he came to visit me for the last time, and now I was telling the whole story again to the Public Prosecutor. The truth in all its details... My meeting with Hans... The way I met Dina... Her seductive proposal for marriage... The mirage of fame and universality that dissipated on her hands... My confrontation with Dina and her insulting me... Sayed and my relationship with him... What I told Sayed... The way he left... His last words... 'So repent to your Creator'... I told Khaled everything... everything.

Finally, after I finished talking, Khaled lit his tenth cigarette and murmured saying, "Hmm... 'So, repent to your Creator and kill yourselves'... God Almighty has spoken the truth. Now I understand! Poor Sayed. He didn't kill Dina to take revenge; he killed her to save you from her trap! Sayed decided that both of you sinned and lost the righteous path, and both of you should repent and pay the price for your repentance as did the owners of the calf when they disobeyed their Prophet Moses, but Sayed decided that you don't have to die because you sinned and followed Dina; he decided to die and let you be, and enough the sacrifice of one sinner."

The interpretation of Khaled to Sayed's last words was brilliant. He was definitely an intelligent person, but that didn't mean that he would be merciful or understanding. I kept my mouth shut, waiting for his verdict.

He continued talking, "Mr. Hamdi, the facts before me indicate that you told Sayed what would encourage him to commit his crime. But they also tell me that you had no intention of harming others. You have been expressing your anger and frustration, and Sayed decided —on his own— to free you from the bondage and humiliation of your wife.

Therefore, the decision, planning and insisting on killing Dina all fall in the hands of the offender alone, and you did not participate in it.

We'll now go to the interrogation room, where I will complete my report and release you. This nightmare will soon be over, and by nightmare I don't mean the interrogation room or this room you are held in; I mean this cruel experience and the vicious atmosphere that doesn't suit you and to which you don't belong."

Khaled pulled his chair to be nearer to me, saying in a low voice, "Hamdi, I am a man who doesn't understand anything about music, but I understand people and know how to weigh them. Hamdi, you are a peaceful man who wants your life to be simple and clear. You play music and people like you, so they ask you to play more and then they like you more and more, and so on. But the society in which you will live in does not follow these simple and clear rules, but rather it despises such rules and belittles them and those who follow them as well. In this society, diligence is trivial and talent is frivolous; even creativity is pointless. For this society, playing politics, slying and lying, and even swindling and deceiving have become good virtues, and the ability to act cunningly, and sometimes even meanly, is far better than any talent or any diligence.

My advice to you is... beware of drifting in the tide of this society. Beware of forgetting your simple, clear rules. Pursue your straight path and never deviate from it, even if you end up playing your music for yourself, alone in your house. For people like you do not stand in front of their mirror to admire their victories and achievements, but rather to hold themselves accountable for their failures and mistakes, and the happiness of those like you lies in how you praise yourself, not how others praise you. So, never, ever, deviate from the straight path you drew for yourself."

The Meeting

"Do you know who the most dangerous people are?"

Khaled and his clerk finished all the paperwork. He gave me an enthusiastic farewell as if we were old friends. I hurried out of the Public Prosecution Office. The first thing I intended to do was to take a long and warm shower and stay under the water for as long as possible. After that, whatever would happen I would let it happen. But that was far away from what would actually happen next...

As soon as I went out into the street, I found two new bulls surrounding me and pushing me into a large car. Who were they that time?! Was this the police again? They couldn't be; their looks and style didn't match with policemen. Neither of them tried to talk to me, nor did I try to ask them. It was clear from their faces that I wouldn't get any answer from them, so I opted for silence.

My confusion did not last long, the car was heading towards Dina's parents' house, the house where I had previously met them to get their blessings; the meeting that lasted only a minute, and the blessing that lasted only a year.

My curiosity turned into panic. The prosecutor, despite having released me, still had many doubts about my participation in the murder of Dina by instigating Sayed. Khaled was sympathetic to my case to the fullest, and that was what enabled me to get out of this predicament. But Dina's father?! His only daughter was killed, and he did not need evidence or proof to assume if I had a role in her killing. The story and the circumstances of what happened were more than enough for a man like him to disprove my innocence and determine my punishment. The man would destroy me without interrogation or investigation! He obviously hated me when I proposed to his daughter, so how would he feel about me when I am accused of killing her?!

We arrived at the house, or what should be called a palace. The two beasts who kidnapped me from the street took me into a room, closed the door, and left.

The room was immensely spacious, all its walls were covered with books, and each had its own luxuriously custom-made cover, a huge library that needed years and years to read everything in it. The bookshelves were separated by several oil paintings, it was clear from the way they were displayed that they were all original paintings by great artists. In the middle, there was a group of antiques and musical instruments scattered in harmony that indicated the elegance and taste of the owner. There was also a Bösendorfer Imperial Concert Grand piano lying in the middle of the room, like the grand jewel of the crown. This was not a reading library; this was a masterpiece of power and influence.

Dina's father was in the room, but he was standing at the far end of it, looking out at the garden through the window with his back towards me. He was as still and silent as an idol, holding his hands behind his back and with his feet slightly apart. The man acted as if he didn't notice my presence, but I could feel his back staring at me! I tried to speak but I couldn't. My mouth was moving but no sound was coming out of my throat. I didn't even think about sitting down, so I ended up standing still like him.

"Did Dina like to listen to you playing the piano?"

I was surprised by the question. I didn't know how to respond. I finally gathered up my courage and said, "Sometimes... sometimes, sir... especially at the beginning of our marriage."

"Which song did she like?"

"She liked the song 'It's hard for me to say I'm sorry' by 'Chicago', and she insisted that I play it for her every day at the beginning of our marriage, especially the intro. It is a beautiful song when played on the piano, so I was..."

The man interrupted my babbling with a gesture from his hand while he was still looking out the window, with his back still staring at me, then he said, "Play this intro for me, please."

**It's hard for me to say
I'm sorry - Chicago**

I sat in front of the piano and started playing. It was a short intro and it didn't take more than half a minute, so it was not long before I stopped playing.

Still, with his back still staring at me, Dina's father continued talking, "Play 'candle in the wind', please."

I began to play this wonderful song composed by Elton John on the eleventh anniversary of Marilyn Monroe's death. It was so beautiful that he sang it again, after some paraphrasing, in mourning for Princess Diana.

Dina's father kept staring at the garden through the window and listening to the music, with his arms behind his back and without the slightest movement, he signalled me after a minute to stop.

**Candle in the wind -
Elton John**

Finally, he turned to me and said, "Thank you. That's enough."

I looked at the man. He looked like a ghost. His face carried the blackness of death, while his eyes were swollen from crying and lack of sleep. I wished he hadn't turned. I wished I kept talking to his back. It was definitely easier than talking to this face that was immersed in sadness.

"Do you know who the most dangerous people are?"

His question took me by surprise. The man was talking about anything and everything but his daughter's murder. I had to be extremely careful with my answers. That man was going to explode in my face at any moment.

"No, sir. I don't."

"The most dangerous person is the one who has nothing to gain and has nothing to lose. You can own any man in the world as long as you know the thing he is eager to win or the thing he is afraid to lose, and so long as you have the power to convince him, or even to delude him, that you can control this thing."

Didn't have the stamina or the courage to talk, so I kept my silence while the man continued talking, "I tried to teach Dina the principles of business and management. After all, she had a whole empire to inherit, but she went after art and sculptures like any idiot who makes idols. She didn't want to go the way I set for her, to become the greatest businesswoman in the region. However, she managed to learn a couple of things from me, and the one thing she learned and mastered was this golden rule: Know what people need or fear, then convince them that you can control this thing. This will give you the power to control and dominate whomever you want."

I wanted to tell him that she rigorously applied this rule with me, and it was what led us to where we were at that moment. But I decided to keep my mouth shut.

Dina's father continued, "The only time that Dina made a mistake in applying this rule was in her dealings with Sayed. She manipulated this poor man until she stripped from him everything that he could be eager to win or afraid to lose. She didn't realize that this poor man would turn on her seeking vengeance, since he had lost everything."

How did he know about Sayed's story and what Dina did to him?! And if he knew, why didn't he stop her? I asked myself those questions, but I didn't dare to ask him. However, he —like his daughter— seemed to know what those around them were thinking about.

"I didn't know about what Dina and this Hani did to Sayed. I knew there was an issue with him in her college a long time ago, and that's it! I just found out the whole story a couple of hours ago. If I had known I would've stopped her. I would've stopped her from destroying this poor man's life."

I was astonished by the man's words ... Not because he seemed to know what his daughter did to Sayed in detail, but because he called Sayed 'the poor man'... twice! He was almost blaming Dina for what happened.

"Sayed did what you didn't and couldn't do."

I jumped off the piano stool with panic surging through me. It seemed that the man had started accusing me of killing his daughter. So I wanted to be ready to defend myself, or to be ready to run! He continued.

"You wished to get rid of Dina, because she destroyed your dreams. She was no longer the paved road nor the ladder that would take you to the fame and glory as you aspired and wished, but she became an obstacle in this path; an obstacle that you had to get rid of."

"Sir! Please. I..."

I didn't finish my sentence... I couldn't... The man shut me up with a thunderous shout in which he put all his anger, "QUIET!"

I froze in my place and didn't reply... I couldn't even breathe... I stood like a statue, frozen by fear, while he came back to his calmness saying, "You wanted to get rid of her. But you, like everyone else like you, wasted your time without doing anything. Sometimes you don't do anything on the pretext that you are planning your biggest strike, and other times you don't do anything on the pretext of following your conscience, other times you don't do anything on the pretext that you are waiting for the right moment. But in the end, you don't do anything."

The man's thunderous shout was still buzzing in my ear, so I kept quiet while he continued talking, "Dina was like me. She rushed to seize opportunities and did whatever she desired momentarily, simply because she loved to win, and she knew that she could get away with anything she did without punishment.

This is because she had it all; money, influence and power. As for those who are like Sayed, they also do as they please; but because they have never tasted victory before. Their lives swing from one loss to a greater loss, so they feel no shame in seizing any opportunity to rebel, they live in a state of constant punishment. As for you, you are the one who danced on the stairs; you didn't do anything and you won't do anything. Passive to the point of hibernation, even to the point of death. You just watch what's around you and think that you are the intelligent, patient and smart one, when in reality you are the hesitant coward."

His words were so humiliating to me that I found myself answering him firmly, saying, "But of the three of us, I am the only one surviving! So, it seems my way—that you don't like—was the best in the end."

The man looked at me and smiled! I expected him to take out a pistol and put a hundred bullets in my chest as a reward for what I just said, or to ask his beasts standing outside to come and chop my head and crush my bones while he would stand there and amusedly watch my body torn to pieces. But the strange thing was that he smiled! And his smile widened little by little until it turned into a raucous laugh. The man continued laughing and laughing as he pointed his finger at me as if he liked what I said.

Finally, he swallowed his laughter and said to me, "Correct! That's right. You are absolutely right. Throughout history this was what actually happened, exactly what you said; the poor and vermin and mob wrestle with the landlords and aristocrats and elite until they destroy each other, while it was those like you who survived."

The man returned to look through the window and contemplate the garden. He remained silent for a while and then said, "Dina knew she was going to die young! She acted all her life with this idea in her mind; she even dealt with us based on the assumption that she would go before any of us. That wasn't the problem; the problem was that we, her mother and I, were feeling the same thing! We always tried not to get too attached to her, because we knew, deep down, that she wouldn't be with us for long."

I didn't know what to say or what to do. The man's words were so full of sadness and grief that it was pointless trying to calm him or even to show sympathy. I said in a stuttering voice, "Sir... I'm sorry for your loss... I wish..."

The man interrupted me and continued his talk as if I was not there.

"Dina left you a lot of money in her will."

I was totally surprised by what he said... Me?! Dina left me money? She cut me back in her life and refused to help me with even a couple of phone calls, and then she was extremely generous in her death, leaving me a fortune like he was saying?! What was wrong with those people?! No, I won't be a part of this charade.

I stood up straight, gathered my courage, and said in a firm voice, "Sir. I don't want money and I don't want an inheritance. This money is not mine and I don't covet it, and here I am returning it to you. If you don't accept it, I will donate it all to charity."

"Well, if you decide to keep it then I will take you to court and sue you for all of it... If you don't agree to give it up, I will force you to give it up."

I quickly replied to him, "No need to threaten me, sir. As I told you, I will give you all your money back voluntarily and immediately."

The man continued talking as if I said nothing, "I am not pushing you to give it up because I want the money, but because that Dina wrote her will so as to make you a partner in our business, which is something that you will not be able to do and will not be acceptable to our partners who will not accommodate a stranger or an intruder ... and this is dangerous for you, if you know what I mean. But still, you will get all the money you want..."

I insisted on interrupting the man so I can defend myself. I wanted to tell him that I married his daughter because I was selfish and greedy, but for glory and not for money.

"Sir, allow me to interrupt you..."

The man turned to me and gave me a fiery look that pushed me back to my seemingly safer silence, while he kept looking at me with eyes that carried all the anger and rage in the world, and said slowly, "Do you know what I would like to do now? I would like to smash your head with a hammer like what happened to my daughter!"

I could feel the blood escaping from my veins, and the cold sweat running down my head. The fiery look he gave me suggested that he would not hesitate for a moment to actually smash my head.

It was no more about if he would kill me or not, it was about how long this conversation would continue before he would actually kill me.

But as suddenly as he threw his threats at me, he retreated and returned to look out the window. It was clear that he was avoiding looking at me so as not to lose his temper and kill me. He started to speak softly and slowly as if he had not threatened to kill me less than a minute ago.

"I will establish a charity in the name of Dina. It will be the largest charity in the country, and under this charity I will sponsor many talented artists who are unable to continue their art studies, and I will announce a scholarship for talented artists to join reputable art schools all over the world, so they can complete their studies abroad."

I gazed at the man with idiotic and dull looks. I didn't know what to say. For the hundredth time in those last couple of days, I didn't know what to say. He continued, "As for you ... you ... you will go to Hans' school, and you will have enough money to buy yourself an opera house, in which you can play your miserable music to yourself if you like."

What the man was telling me was simply above and beyond my understanding or my expectations. So I decided to remain in my silent corner till the end. I kept my idiotic lull, and he kept talking, "You will continue your studies as you wish, and you will become a great artist as Dina expected you to be... and the first piece of music you will compose will be in her name... Dina."

I was astonished with what the man was saying, but the peak of my surprise was when he said 'A great artist as Dina expected you to be'! Was Dina predicting a bright future for me?! The last thing she said to me was that I had a shallow talent and limited capabilities!

Dina's father continued talking.

"On the piano, you will find a business card with my lawyer's numbers on it. Call him at any time and he will solve any problem you face. He has instructions to do that."

The man's voice started to tremble and quaver with sadness.

"You will also find on the piano a letter addressed to your name... Dina left it to you with her will...

Please... don't read it now... Wait till you go to Hans' school..."

The man turned to me, with his eyes overflowing with tears, and sobbingly said, "And then you will know... why I didn't smash your head."

The Glory

"Fate snatched Hassan from my arms, and here it was giving me Malak."

The man went to a side door, opened it and left, leaving me alone with hurricanes and storms of conflicting thoughts and feelings, and leaving me with more questions than answers. How did Dina call me shallow, untalented, and then tell her father that she expected me to be a great artist? How did this man carry so much hatred towards me that he wanted to smash my head, and then pour money down on me like waterfalls? How could he accuse me of killing his daughter and then send me to Hans's School, fulfilling the dream of my life? Is there something I did not understand for my stupidity and lack of intelligence, or did this whole family belong not to the realm of the sane, but to the world of the insane?!

I opened the door and found the two beasts waiting for me. They took me in the car to my old house and then set off. As soon as I opened the door and went inside, I remembered poor Sayed; The world turned over for the death of Dina, and everyone forgot the death of her killer. It's a nasty world that respects only the rich and powerful, even when they die.

I decided to forget the past, all the past, and to think about what was to come.

Only minutes passed after I entered the house until my phone started ringing. It was a number from Austria.

"Hello, Mr. Hamdi."

It was Hans... damned! Now he remembered me! He even talked to me himself. He must have received the orders to help me! But I couldn't blame him. He was playing along so his school could continue. We are all slaves to our needs one way or the other.

Hans began speaking English with a heavy Austrian accent,

"I hope you are doing well, and excuse me for the delay. It has been a year since we met. I wanted to call you earlier but there were many problems that stopped me from doing so. Now all our problems have been solved. So, my question to you is: Do you still want to join my school?"

"Yes, sir."

"Great! I'll give you a month to get your stuff together and get ready to travel, I'll send you your plane ticket and the rest of the information you need. You better start training now! There is a lot of hard work waiting for you here, and we have a lot to do..."

"Two tickets! please send two tickets."

I interrupted Hans, who was totally surprised by my request for two tickets instead of one. A minute of silence passed, then he said, "Mr. Hamdi. Will you have company on this trip? You know the schools' strict policy about this."

"The ticket is for another student who will join your school."

Malak... It was Malak I was thinking of, the beautiful piano butterfly. Her name bounced in my mind while talking to Hans. Despite those great events and successive waves of shocks I was in the midst of, I haven't stopped thinking of her. I loved this girl; my little sister and her sharp mind. She pulled me out of her mother's arms and from the clutches of my despair and despondency, and I ought to pull her out of the brothel she lived in with that mother of hers. I should give her the chance she deserved, I would take care of that girl and help her become a Grandmaster one day, paving her way for the glory she deserved. The path that I always sought after and always slipped away from me. I would not let her suffer the whims of her mother, nor let her talent go to waste. And if we could not continue our relationship as a piano teacher and student, let us continue it as classmates and peers.

"Mr. Hamdi. Can you hear me?"

Hans's voice over the phone interrupted my thoughts of Malak, but didn't take me away from the decision I just made.

"Yes, Mr. Hans. Sorry, I lost you for a moment, but I can hear you now. Yes, as I mentioned to you; there will be another student who will come with me to join your school."

"Mr. Hamdi. This is not the way things are run here. Our school has its own way..."

I quickly responded by saying, "She is a talented artist, I assure you. She's young enough to be shaped and trained, with great aptitude and ability to train for hours upon hours, and she is a great material for a Grandmaster project. Hear her and decide for yourself, and I'm sure she will exceed your expectations, and if you don't find her to be the right material for a professional musician, then let her join your school anyway, and I will bear all the expenses. I think you know now that I have enough money to do that."

Hans burst into a long laugh and said, "Okay, Mr. Hamdi. I will listen to her if you truly believe in her. I trust your judgment on others' talent as much as I trust yours. Let's set a time to listen to her playing, and let it be next week. And if I find her as talented as you say I will offer her a full scholarship, just like you."

The call ended. And for the first time since the death of my brother Hassan, I felt the taste of true joy. I felt a strange warmth running through my being, reaching my heart to wash it and my brain to enlighten it. For the first time since forever I felt that peaceful and calm.

Fate snatched Hassan from my arms, and here it was giving me Malak. I failed to keep Hanan as a sister, so let me be a brother to Malak, this delicate golden-brained butterfly.

I was sure Malak wouldn't mind; her heart would leap up for joy by this opportunity. She would be learning the piano that she loved, all the way to becoming a professional pianist. She would be joining the club of great musicians and would stay away from her mother and her foolish behavior. The only obstacle was Ingie. How could I persuade her to let Malak travel with me? And most importantly, how could she be persuaded to let Malak travel alone and get out of her life?

Suddenly, I found the words of Dina's father echoing in my mind, 'You own any person in the world as long as you know what he or she is eager to win or is afraid to lose, and as long as you have the power to convince, or even to delude, him or her that you can control that thing.' It was actually a great rule to learn when dealing with others, and if I have failed to coexist with millionaires, then at least I could learn something from their tricks. Let Ingie be my guinea pig, and let me try this golden rule with her.

* * * *

A week later, I was with Ingie in the annex. She rushed to my arms and showered me with her kisses.

"Where have you been, you damned?! I missed you so much."

Ingie grabbed my hand and pulled me to the bed, but I gently pulled my hand from hers and said to her, "Ingie. There is no time for that now. There is an important topic to discuss."

Ingie's face showed fear. She was the type of person who didn't like surprises but rather was terrified by them, and this was one of her weaknesses I intended to use.

"Ingie. There is a golden opportunity for Malak, an opportunity that only very few in the millions of pianists in the world can catch, an opportunity of a lifetime."

Ingie didn't talk. She looked at me with the same astonished looks I gave to Dina's father. So, I continued talking.

"There is a school in Vienna for talented pianists, which I myself am about to join to continue my studies. The graduates of this school have only one place to embrace them, which is the top! This school is considered the fast track for becoming a professional pianist, and the cornerstone of approaching the title of Grandmaster pianist. I talked to the school owner about Malak and about her talent and aptitude, and he is willing to accommodate her as one of the students. A full stay in Vienna for three years, after which she'll begin her professional career."

Ingie jumped like a cat ready to attack, she threw me with fiery looks and said in an angry voice, "And what do you have to do with anything related to Malak?! You are merely her piano tutor. She is my daughter, and she will stay with me here."

"Ingie, please try to understand. This is the opportunity of a lifetime, your daughter will have the greatest future you can ever wish for her, and I know how much you love her and wish her all the best."

Ingie kept silent for a moment, then looked at me defiantly and said, "If I agreed to what you are saying, it would be on one condition, that I live with her in Vienna."

"Ingie. The school during the three years of study requires full dedication from its students; no family and no friends, only continuous training, so there is no place for you there."

"Then it won't happen. I don't agree, and please don't talk about this again."

I looked at Ingie pretending to be sad. I stood up slowly and got an envelope out of my pocket. I looked at the envelope and said calmly to her, "I was expecting that from you. Unfortunately, it's not your decision; it's the decision of Malak... and her father!"

Ingie jumped up, standing on the bed she was sitting on, screaming,

"And what does her bloody father have to do with all of this? The custody of Malak is with me, and I am the one responsible for any decision concerning her. This fool has no opinion or right to interfere, so do not try to involve him in something that does not concern him."

I started waving the envelope in my hand as I calmly replied.

"The custody is with you now, but it won't stay with you for long when Malak's father finds out about your relationship with me... with Medhat Salem, the tennis coach... and Dr. Helmy your neighbor... and the rest of the names on this list! And when I put, in his hands and the hands of his lawyer, this evidence that

I have collected over the past days, which indicate that you are hosting men here in your home under the sight and hearing of his daughter, he will surely win custody! There is no judge in the world who would agree to leave such an innocent girl in the hands of a reckless mother like you."

Ingie's legs trembled, and she fell on the bed crying and sobbing.

"Malak knows nothing... I don't care about her father... Malak knows nothing... Never say anything to her... You bastard... You wretch!"

I approached her and gently patted her shoulder, saying, "Why are you throwing these bad words at me, Ingie?! I came to offer you and your daughter the opportunity of a lifetime, and you curse me?! Malak will be one of the most famous pianists in the world, and you will be the great mother who sacrificed everything for her and for her future. She will adore you for the sacrifices you will make for her, and you will spend your lives together moving between the theaters of Paris and New York. I deserve kisses, you crazy woman... kisses not curses."

Ingie looked at me desperately, with her beautiful eyes full of tears and a shivering smile on her lovely face.

She gave up, and I won; I won because I followed the golden rule of Dina's father. Ingie loved her daughter, hated her husband and was afraid of scandal. And I played on all these points so that I could make her accept what I imposed on her. The lesson I learned from Dina's father was great; it was greater than all my piano lessons.

I left the annex to herald Malak of the success of my plan. I put the envelope back in my pocket, it was an envelope containing a couple of music sheets from the opera Aida!

Ingie agreed, and Malak the butterfly flew out of joy, hugging her mother and hugging me, calling her friends laughing to tell them how happy she was then calling them crying because she would miss them. She was giggling, weeping, talking a lot and keeping her mouth shut... all at the same time! She asked me about the weather in Vienna and the clothes she should take with her, then decided that she will not leave the school for the whole three years. She asked me for extensive training before traveling, then begged me to stop the lessons and have enough rest before we travel. Eager to start but terrified of the experience, ready to meet Hans but evading his call! The beautiful, innocent butterfly with her golden brilliant mind.

* * * *

Days have passed quickly; Malak and I were training every day for hours. Ingie was only sitting with us for a few minutes then she would leave, her tight and revealing clothes were gone, her Nat Sherman cigarettes were gone, and with them was the slutty nightgown.

Two days before traveling, Ingie came to sit with us. She opened one of her magazines and went through its pages, then suddenly she interrupted our training to say, "Malak. I asked a contractor to come and check the garden. I will take down the annex, I do not need it. I will build a shed for shade plants in its place. I love taking care of plants and flowers. You know that gardening was always my favorite hobby, and I want to go back to it."

Ingie looked at me after she had finished her words. She was trying to send me a message with these words; she wanted to inform me of her repentance, and that she would never host men again in the annex. I was the one meant to hear those words, she wanted to assure me that she would not do anything that would disgrace Malak, and that taking down the annex was a sign of her sincere repentance and her new beginning.

At this moment, the most unexpected thing happened. Malak rose and rushed with all her might to hug her mother, with her eyes welling with tears. Malak, with her clever golden mind, understood her mother's message to me, and realized that her mother had decided to walk away from the path of sinfulness, taking down her mistakes with the annex. The tender butterfly realized it all, and flew with joy into the arms of her repentant mother.

Ingie also realized... realized that Malak knew everything... realized that she knew what was going on in the annex, and that she preferred silence and concealment so as not to injure her mother. At this moment, Ingie burst into tears as well, a cry forced by feelings of repentance and regret mixed with joy and hope. Ingie held Malak so tight in her arms and showered her with kisses. Malak laughed and cried at the same time, and kept wiping her mother's tears with her tender hands.

That scene brought back the memory of my brother... and my mother... and my family. My tears fell silently yet profusely. They were tears of joy and contentment; tears that I had never known before. I gathered my feelings oscillating between satisfaction and sadness... and left the villa.

The Letter

"Money may be of use to you along the way... but would not do me any good where I will end up."

From that moment, it was all hard work. For Malak and myself, we spent hours and hours of training and had only a few minutes to rest. But these hours felt like seconds for us. It seemed that our eagerness and ambition had made us lose the sense of time. Days passed so quickly as if it was Murray Perahia was in charge of heavenly clock. Hans took care of all the documents and logistics of our trip, and Ingie took care of all our needs while training, allowing us to focus on one thing; the piano.

Murray Perahia

Finally, on the plane. We were about to take off. The innocent Malak was jumping on the plane seat like a butterfly and couldn't settle in one place. She was happy with the experience, happy with the opportunity, happy with the challenge that awaited her and the promising future ahead. As for me, my mind was thinking only about one thing... the letter... the letter that Dina's father gave me. He told me to read it only when I got to school, and I was on the plane that was about to take off. I thought it was okay for me now to read it. I reached my pocket. I took out the letter, unfolded the envelope, and started reading.

"My beloved Hamdi. Yes, you are my beloved. Hamdi... I love you... I love you without reason or justification... I have loved you since the first moment I saw you. I love your naivety and simplicity. I love your devotion to your art and your faith in your talent. I love everything about you.

If you read this letter, it means that I have died. I know for sure that my life will be short. I don't know how long it will be or when it will end.

All I know is that my life will be short and painful, and that my end will be bloody and even more painful. I don't know why I picture my life and my death in this gloomy and dark way. All I know is that this is what will definitely happen. And here my thoughts have come true... and the proof is that you are reading this letter now.

I'm sick, Hamdi. I don't know how to love! I don't know how to show my affection or how to express my feelings to others. I don't have a physical disease. My parents didn't torture me when I was young; they didn't deprive me of anything. My childhood was beautiful and quiet, so I can't find a reason for my illness. All I know is that I don't know how to love, or —to be more clear— I don't know how to express love.

The more I love a person, the more I find myself indulging in torturing and harming him, and enjoying his suffering and pain, and the greater and deeper my love is, the keener I am to torture and hurt the one I love... and I loved you with all my heart, that's why I hurt you with all my heart. I showed you coldness and indifference because I knew how much it hurt you.

I kept you from continuing your path and honing your talent because I knew that that was all you were striving to achieve. I was doing all of that and then I would go to my room, close the door and slap myself on the face and curse myself in the dark... I was punishing myself because I was punishing you... and I was punishing you because I love you.

I have made many mistakes and committed many sins in my life, including what inevitably entitles me to eternity in hell, and I know that and accept it. It is the evils with which I harmed others returning back to haunt me, and it is the hatred I carried in my heart coming back to hunt me. And there is no room for mercy for those like me, and no room for forgiveness for those who did my deeds.

All I ask of you, Hamdi, is that you forgive me... forgive me for everything I have done to hurt you. Forget the domineering, tyrannical Dina, and just remember the Dina who loved you... Dina who wrote this letter... the sick Dina; the poor woman who was not able to practice the simplest degrees of humanism, which is to show love and exchange feelings.

Forgive me, Hamdi, and go on your way. Continue your life without me. Don't look behind. Seek your way to glory because it is definitely what you deserve. You are gifted, so don't let anyone stop you from reaching your glorious goal... I won't be with you on this path... but, please, allow me to help you with the only thing I have... money. Keep your future in mind and let me make up for the pain I have caused you with money, the money that may be of use to you along the way... but would not do me any good where I will end up.

Forgive me, Hamdi. Forgive me, my love. But the most important thing is to forgive yourself... Don't blame yourself for marrying me... Don't look at our relationship as a fault or a mistake... Rather, see it as a lesson... a piano lesson."

*** *The End* ***

About the Author

Keep in touch with Ashraf via the web:

e-mail: ashraf2183@yahoo.com

Website: https://www.peakupnow.com/

Facebook: http://www.facebook.com/peakupnow

Instagram: https://instagram.com/ashibrahim125/

Dr. Ashraf Ibrahim is a physician by education, a business consultant by profession, and an author by passion. He has several literary works as well as books and publications in the field of human development and business communication, in which he reveals new visions and methods for success in life based on his experiences and visions in this field.

He holds a Bachelor degree of Medicine and Surgery from Faculty of Medicine, Alexandria University, year 1993. He worked in the field of medicine, healthcare industry, and business consultancy. He currently resides in Canada.

His passion for writing extended to fiction. His first novel, "The Piano Lesson" was published in March 2021 in his native language. It attracted the attention and admiration of readers, became an Amazon best seller, and went for a second print in October 2021. The author decided to introduce "The Piano Lesson" in English as well.

Ashraf carries over twenty-five years of experience in the field of business and individual performance management. He utilizes his extensive life experience, gained through working with patients, healthcare professionals and people from all the over world for over a quarter of a century, to serve his writings and his literary works, fiction and non-fiction.

Published by the Author

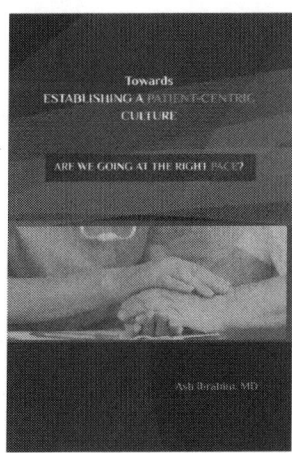

PEAK UP ... NOW!

This book features practical and real-life guidelines for fulfilling your potential and achieving success and growth within your organization.

The chapters are based on the rich experience I have built, working in and with organizations for over twenty-five years.

The primary aim of this book is to provide you with the recipe for success that helps you navigate your way within a corporate setting, and it's packed with examples, rationale, and well-tested techniques of application.

PEAK UP mixes literature with business, by introducing the story of Adam and Eve, and how Adam is progressing in his life and his career, based on the advices and support of his dedicated mentor, Eve. This approach makes the book quite attractive and interesting to follow, adapting a new approach that is away from the dry and rigid approach to business issues.

The PASS

Studies show that teaching assertiveness in the workplace is effective in developing skill, but is not effective in improving interpersonal relations or reducing business conflicts. This means that becoming assertive in the usual fashion can help us fight our battles in the workplace, but it can also cause us to lose the whole war in the end. The problem is that we keep trying to be more assertive without learning how to use this assertiveness to our best interest.

Most assertiveness workbooks jump to teach us to be more assertive in the workplace without telling us how, when, and to what extent to use this critical communication skill. This is why I routinely watched many people—across my twenty-five years of corporate experience—using assertiveness to speak up, only to find themselves going down!

In this book, The PASS, I will address this highly critical and extremely sensitive topic, which is interpersonal communication skills in organizations. I will start by helping you develop the assertive mentality that guides your business communication. I will help you develop the assertive behaviour to reflect your self-confidence and professionalism even before you talk, then—and only then—I will present several unique assertiveness techniques, including my state-of-art assertive message model, that proved to be a great asset in our day-to-day communication in the workplace.

EVALYOUATE!

65% of the studies that compared self-rated assessments with external observations among professionals demonstrate little or no relation between both. Meaning we have difficulty conducting a well-structured, balanced and objective self-assessment. Fortunately, there are effective tools to help us realize our capabilities and assess our own strengths and weaknesses.

«EVALYOUATE!» will guide you to: 1) assess your successes and challenges and link them to your capabilities; 2) see the bigger picture of your capabilities and its impact on your work performance; and 3) set the basis for planning your own self- improvement goals and how to work on them. All are critical factors for your success and career growth.

Most books that discuss self-assessment focus on the "why"; they stress the importance of self-evaluation and the value of understanding your own strengths and capabilities. EVALYOUATE discusses the "how"; it introduces an easy to follow, step-by- step scheme that helps you realize your strengths and assess your weaknesses using a systematic approach to help you fully understand your capabilities.

FEED-FORWARD

In one survey that involved almost 900 people, 92% of respondents agreed with the assertion, "Negative feedback, if delivered appropriately, is effective at improving performance." We seem to know the importance of feedback, and realize how it can be of great value in improving our performance. Still, we rely on those providing us with feedback to deliver it appropriately.

We're waiting for others to be positive, constructive, and extremely tactful in their feedback they're giving us. But, what if they're not? What if their feedback was lacking tactfulness, or too direct, vague, or not so considerate? Should we drop this feedback simply because it was not delivered to us in the way we see appropriate?

"Feed-forward" is about using each and every piece of feedback we receive to improve our own future performance. "Feed-forward" is about developing the mindset that embraces, encourages, and elicits feedback rather than deflecting it. It's about developing the discipline and determination to turn this feedback-embracing mindset and feedback-verifying skill into a clear and structured process that has only one way to take us... forward.

Questions from the book club

1. The idea of QR codes is totally new. This is the first time we see it in a novel? How did you come up with this idea?

   The challenge was for me to make the reader believe that Hamdi is a great pianist with the talent and skills of a Grandmaster to-be. I tried to deliver this message from the first page through his description of his favourite music 'La Campanella'. However, I had the challenge of making the reader listen to this marvellous piece of music at the same time he or she was reading about so they can realize what Hamdi was talking about, and hence came the idea of using the QR code. Watching the music played on YouTube will allow readers not only to listen to it, but also to realize how difficult it is to play, and this is what I want to deliver.

   I used it throughout the book because I felt it would be a great opportunity to make the readers more familiar with the names and the composers of some of the famous pieces of music that they listen to in their regular life without knowing their names or the names of their composers. I strongly believe that fiction writing can extend to be more educational by adding some facts and general information that give more knowledge to the readers and more value to their work.

2. "The Piano Lesson" is great, but it is short! I personally enjoyed reading it. However, I felt at certain points that I needed to learn more; learn about the characters like Hassan and Hanan, learn about Ihab ... Why didn't you extend your novel to talk more about these characters?

This is the story of Hamdi and his struggle. And all the other characters mentioned in the story are there because their interaction with Hamdi participated in shaping his life to the way it became. For a novel, I believe that any other details for those characters will not be necessary. However, it is these characters that will enrich the scenario of "The Piano Lesson" when, hopefully, it is turned into a movie.

Second, I'm a big fan of short stories. I believe writing short fictions requires a special type of talent and skill; it is the talent of delivering several messages between the lines, and making readers know, see and feel things without directly mentioning them. And this is the way I tried to follow when writing "The Piano Lesson". One of the things that makes me so happy is when a reader tells me that he or she read my work twice or three times in a raw, this means that they realized the messages hidden between the lines.

3. How long did it take you to write "The Piano Lesson"?

Two months for writing it, two months earlier for research and collecting materials, and over forty years of accumulating life experiences.

4. Wow! Do you believe that a good writer must have this extensive life experience before he or she can introduce their work to readers?

I'm not saying it's a must; but experience is definitely a great asset for those who have it. I believe that writing in general is about the synthesis of knowledge, and this synthesis of knowledge requires not only experience, but also the ability to learn from this experience and to translate it into something creative and unique.

5. Did your medical background help you when building the character of Dina?

Definitely it did. However, it was my real-life experiences and encounters with several people who were more or less like Dina that helped me shape the character the way I did. I was so happy with the calls I received and the discussions I had with several psychiatrists who read the novel and wanted to discuss the characters of Dina and Hamdi with me. Without exposing the details of the novel, there were

a couple of points where Dina didn't act exactly by the book; meaning she showed actions and behaviour that doesn't match her diagnosis. This is something I learned from my experience, which is that there is no single person with psychiatric disorder will show exactly all the symptoms and signs stated in the medical textbooks. This is because simply we are not 'cases'; we are human beings.

6. Did you find difficulty translating "The Piano Lesson" from Arabic to English?

It was quite difficult in the beginning, but once I realized the difference in styles between both it was a smooth process.

7. What are your coming projects?

I'm launching the rest of my English business books by December 2021. I wanted to learn more about book publishing and marketing before publishing them, now I think I'm ready. However, that doesn't mean I will be away from fiction writing, I will be working on translating my second novel to the English language as well.

8. Have you received questions before about the clash of social classes in your novel?

Yes, and it makes me so happy when I get such questions. It means that my key message is delivered to the reader, although it was never mentioned explicitly in the novel. Dina, Hamdi and Sayed... each represent one of the social classes forming our society, and their struggle through out the story reflects the struggle of these three classes in our society to survive and advance. We can definitely run a reading session in the club where we can highlight certain parts in the story and discuss how they are representing what was above and beyond their individual characters.

9. Do you think you could establish yourself as a fiction writer through "The Piano Lesson"?

It is still a long way to go. And I still have lots of things to do before I can say so. However, "The Piano Lesson" helped me establish a strong base of friends and supporters who read the novel and are got quite attached to it. I can tell you that "The Piano Lesson" has reached more than five countries in Asia, Africa and Europe, not through a publisher or a distributor, but through those readers who helped me getting my novel available in their countries. This tells me that I am on the right track of establishing myself as a fiction writer.

10. Which character is the closest to your heart?

I understand where Hamdi is coming from. This is because I was in his shoes; I was raised in a middle-class family that entrenched the concepts of "right and wrong" and "black and while" in my brother and I. We were raised on the simple rule that right is right and wrong is wrong, and that's it. However, when I started my professional career, especially in the multinational organizations, I started to feel that it was all gray! And that your real skill is not to differentiate between black and white, but rather to know how to 'play' in the gray area without drowning into your own sins.

I feel so sympathetic for Dina. She's sick, and there was no one there to help her. Not because they didn't care, but because they just couldn't. Her case of narcissism was so advanced that no one could help her. That's why I feel sorry for her; but that doesn't mean that I agree with any of her wrong doings.

Made in the USA
Las Vegas, NV
27 December 2021